The Wrigh

The Perfect Love Strangers

By

Benji the Wrighter

Published by The Wrighter's Block

Benji the Wrighter, 43 Craft Street, Cincinnati, Ohio 45232 U.S.A.

Copyright © Benji the Wrighter, 2020

All rights reserved

Printed in the United States of America

Designed by Benji the Wrighter and JPVisuals

Publisher's Note

This is a work of fiction, Names, characters, places and incidents either are the products of the author's imagination or are used fictitiously and any resemblance to actual persons, living or dead, events or locales is entirely coincidental.

Without limiting the rights under copyright reserved above, no part of this publication may be reproduced, stored in or introduced into a retrieval system, or transmitted in any form, or by any means (electronic, mechanical, photocopying, recording or otherwise), without the prior written permission of both the copyright owner(s) and the above publisher of this book.

Acknowledgements

First, I want to thank God for giving me my gift and the strength to do it. I want to thank my brother, Ronnie, for all the calls and messages asking about the progress and even coming to the house, checking in on me to make sure I was in a good mindset. Thank you for yanking me out the house when I didn't want to leave out the house wanting to rush the book. Aunt Tisha, thank you for being there when I had a meltdown, for all the hot meals, countless messages with Ronnie, encouraging me to keep going and helping me with her when I needed a break! Kuzin Ron Don, thank you for being there to push me back in the push me back in the ring when I wanted to stop. Thank you for appreciating my art and being there to help me understand my gift. Dear Grandma, thank you for the knowledge of the business world and God. You implemented Him in me from birth and I thank you! With the business aspect, I wouldn't be here if it wasn't for you and Grandpa. Mrs. Edmondson, thank you so much for gracing me with editorial services to strengthen this body of work. NIKKILOSPHY!!! Sis, thank you so much for your rndless support! Jaylen! My dear brother, the life you gave my book with that talented eye of yours! I'm forever grateful! My #Wrighter's! Thank you, thank you, THANK YOU! Thank you for being there, encouraging me to keep the dream alive

Chapter One

The Start of It All

As I wake up on our moving day, it excites me that we are moving back to my hometown, Cincinnati. I've been so happy about this day because I finally get to move back to my old stomping grounds to attend the University of Cincinnati. I've been waiting for this day for the longest, although moving means I have to leave my BFF's: Briana, Christina and Bryant. I think about them as I finish loading up the truck, my heart breaking. After placing the last box onto the truck, I return to my room one last time, the emptiness creates an echo from my feet. Tired from hauling boxes, I sit on the floor of my room and look out the window. A few minutes later there is a light tap on my door.

"Who is it?" I ask.

"It's us," I hear a very familiar voice say.

"Come in." My door instantly opens up to Briana, Christina and Bryant looking all gloomy eyed. They know how sensitive I am, especially when it comes to saying good-byes.

"So today is the big day, huh?" Briana asks.

"I guess so, huh?" I reply with.

Right then and there, we grabbed each other and began to cry. We've been friends since I had been living in Birmingham. Within the little time we've known each other, they've been there with me through the thick and thin.

"Ima really miss you guys. I mean who am I gonna call to go shopping with before school starts?" I say in my dramatic way, but my friends are used to it. If I can't be dramatic then I can't be me. "It's my entire fault because I just had to get accepted to the University of Cincinnati. I must say I think my mama ain't really feeling it" I look down at the floor and sigh.

"Is it because of the history with your father, Demonte?" Brianna asked.

Before we lived in the beautiful city of Birmingham, we lived in the wonderful suburbs of Cincinnati. My father really abused my mother, brother, and me, Demonte Durrell Bryant. My brother, Trey, and I went through a lot together when we were younger and I guess that's why we are really close. I really do think it's hard for her because my father was very abusive towards her. He used to beat her for no reason but she chose to stay. When I was younger, I never understood why she did that anyway because that's not real love, I thought.

Then I met someone who made the whole situation clearer or maybe I learned my lessons well from my mother, I always was a quick study. Maybe that is why I stayed so long with my ex-boyfriend, Ryan. Ryan stands about 6 foot 5 inches, has flawless dark skin with a body built like a gladiator. What did he say to get Demonte's attention? We met about a year ago at "The Edge" Movie Theater when both of us were attending the premiere showing of "Obsessed". I know, I know. I should've taken the hint to not get involved, but I chose not to. The first six months were bliss, but in the seventh month, the whole fake Ryan disappeared and his true self came out. That is when he started to beat me and that's when I couldn't take it anymore.

At first, Ryan was so perfect and nice. He always made sure that I was okay financially and emotionally ok. He would take me out on dates, take me out on little rondevu's but then that's when he changed for the worse. He would beat me for the little things like if he felt that I was checking out other guys or going out on dates with Bryant. It was hard for me to explain the bruises to my mother and dear God to Trey. I would have to try my best to keep Trey under control because he would always be ready to fight for his little brother.

"I guess. I just hope we just can keep the negative part of our past in the past, including Ryan," I say in a depressed sigh.

"Well, look at it this way. You'll be able to start over in a somewhat unfamiliar place," Julia starts to say.

"But look, we wish you the best, but me and Christina gotta jet." So, they gave me one last hug before leaving me in the room alone with Brian. Things started to feel uncomfortable, but natural at the same time. I just want to start apologizing for ever choosing Ryan over him, but the past is the past, right?

I really don't know why I chose Ryan over Brian. I guess it was the body or maybe the way he looked at me with those big brown eyes. It wasn't long before, maybe two weeks, Ryan and I became official, which I know killed Brian on the inside.

"Demonte, why? Do you know how it hurt me when you pranced around here with him?" he asks.

"I really don't know Brian, I don't. I wish I could take it back, but I can't."

We look at each other, dead in the eye which made me burst into tears. I have to admit that I kind of did play but I couldn't afford to jeopardize our relationship as friends.

"Do you know how much I suffered watching you 'love' him? If you would just say you love me, I'll forget the fact that you left me for him," he pleads. "Just let me hear you say those three little words, PLEASE!"

"Brian, you know I do, so why are you tripping? Things got kind of complicated for us, then I got scared and ran from you to him. What else can I say to convince you that I love you?" I plead.

"Look, I gotta go but promise me you won't forget about me and you. That's all I ask," he says to me. We just stood looking at each other in the eye as if we had more to say but, as usual, nothing came out. I never and I mean NEVER felt this numb in front of him before. When he turned to leave I grabbed his arm, pulling him into me for a hug. A hug that was so firm, tight and long that I could tell our heart beats at the same time.

"Look, I really gotta go because I'm running super late. Just know I will always love you no matter what," he says.

Just like that, he was out of my room and my house, and it felt like my life. I swear I wish there was more said than what was said because I know he had a lot more to say. As I stood there, I literally lost it thinking about what it could have been between us. I had not cried this hard in a long time and when I heard his car pull off it made it worst.

"Damn, why me?" I ask myself. That's all I could think while I try to pull myself together. I went into the bathroom to try to clean myself and that's when I heard my brother roll over in his room, just now waking up, grumpy and all. All I can think about was my lifestyle. I just wonder if my mother and brother know that I'm gay. I mean I've always had everything under control with faking this life just for them. I wanna tell them but I'm afraid they won't accept me. Briana keeps telling me to sit them down and talk to them, but I could never get the nerve to do it.

I finally am done in the bathroom, then I hear a knock on our front door which made me look out of the window. It's Ryan. I swear the room started to spin around in circles because I really didn't wanna see him before I left. I rushed around in my empty room putting on the clothes I left on. "Why today? Why did he have to pop up out the blue and ruin what could've been a great start of a new life?" I question myself. Why is he here? I'm pretty sure I made it clear that I didn't wanna see him beforehand. My life just keeps getting better and better by the minute. I think my mom still doesn't know that Ryan and I went together or if she does, she hasn't said a mumbling word about it. I finally hear a knock on my door which made me jump and then I see Ryan's figure coming through the door.

"Hey, Demonte. I know we agreed to not to see each other before you left but I couldn't resist", Ryan says.

"Look, why are you really here? And please spare me the bull this time because I have a lot of things to do, like starting a new life without you", I say. I know I'm harsh but Ryan messed up a good thing in his life and I believe he sees that now.

"Why do you always have to start an argument, Demonte? You know how much I love you, but when we were together, I was going through some things."

"Here we go again, Ryan. So, let me guess, those black eyes and bruises were part of you going through it too, huh?" I ask.

"But Demonte, I need you in my life bad. Baby, please don't leave me."

Okay, now this is a low blow to the heart. It's like he thinks if he begs, I'll take him back which will never happen. In the middle of the middle of his plead barging, I hear a knock on the door.

"Hate to cut it short but, Demonte, we'll be pulling off soon, okay?" my mother says. Thank God for my impatient mother because I was getting tired of him begging.

"Okay, I'll be right down", I say to her. She closes the door and I look back at Ryan who has on his sad face. I look at the floor, the empty room, anywhere but at those eyes that make me melt. I don't' feel sorry for him. It only reminds me of the beatings and I begin to get angry. "Look I gotta go so if you don't mind leaving, that'll be great". Call me heartless or whatever you wanna call me but I'M DONE!

"I'll go but we're not over just yet", he says making a beeline to my front door.

Just then my brother was walking out of his room with his duffel bag looking at me funny.

"What was that all about?" he asks.

"I don't know but I do know I'm ready to leave Birmingham," I reply.

"Y'all ready to roll out because I'm trying to beat traffic?" my mother shouts from the truck. I can hear her slamming down the door.

"Man, let's go before she snaps."

We are both chuckling towards the door when it finally hits me that this is the moment where I could redo my whole life over from here on out. I'm finally able to walk out this house of misery with a little peace. I finally get to the car with the hope of starting a new life without stress.

Chapter Two

How We Meet

We're on our way back to Cincinnati, which is a long ride; it's draining me but we're almost there. With a few pit stops, we made it there in ten hours, which was cool with me. When we finally arrive believe it or not it was kind of hot and muggy. I don't know though; it just might be what the doctor ordered in order for me to get my life together. When we crossed over the bridge from Kentucky into Cincinnati I gasped. The city's skyline is so beautiful at night.

"Okay, Gentlemen. Do you know what you want to eat?" my mother asks.

"Sure. I want McDonald's though," I say.

"Man, you always want McDonald's and plus I don't want McDonald's. Can I get Wendy's?" he asks.

"Sure, why not?" So as we make our way around to our different restaurants, we enjoy laughs and a lot of sightseeing before we officially make our way to the new house.

Since we had a little daylight left, we did a little tour of the house and sorted the rest of the stuff. Man, I never knew that moving was so stressful but I enjoyed it. We finally got done sorting and I started unpacking. I took a nice long shower that my body was begging for. When I dried myself off, got dressed and stood out on the back balcony, which is over our back porch, I see a shirtless figure running through the path in the park. From what I can see he had a pretty nice body that was covered in sweat. It looked like he worked out often which I like because I'm more of a gym rat but I can make some adjustments. I stayed outside a little more with my notebook and pen writing some more poetry to relieve some stress. This really helped me when dealing with Ryan's baggage. Suddenly I hear the sliding door open and it turned out to be my beloved brother.

"You ok out here, Young Buck?" he asks.

"Yeah, just relieving some stress, that's all. You know, Trey, I really love writing. I mean, I REALLY LOVE writing, but I know that right now it's not going pay the bills," I start telling him but he stops me.

"Look, Dee, I got your back 100%, know that. Listen to your heart because at the end of the day, if you're not happy there's no point in doing it," he says.

I never knew my brother had it in him to say all this, which touches me.

"But look, let me get in here and get some sleep before work in the morning. Good night," he says.

"Trey, thanks," I say.

"Anytime," he says before disappearing in the house.

So, I finally go in after writing, so hard and furious that my fingertips are numb. I find my mother in the kitchen drinking tea.

"What were you doing outside, sweetie?" she asks.

"The usual, writing poetry and enjoying the city air. Now I'm about to head to bed."

My mother can never go to bed without drinking a cup of hot tea, even in the summer. She swears it soothes her before bed but I never had the interest to try it.

"Okay," she sips and looks thoughtful. "I'm thinking Chinese food for dinner tomorrow. Is that okay with you?"

"Yeah sure."

"Okay, well go get some sleep because you have a long day tomorrow," she says.

"Ok. Good night, Ma."

I got to my room, picking up my phone from the dresser to check my messages. I see that Ryan blew my phone up with calls. I just simply ignored it all because there was nothing to talk about and I really didn't wanna talk to him anyway. So I decided to text the crew back home to let them know we okay and told Julia to call me in the morning sometime. I finally got under my covers thinking about the guy I saw tonight. I just wanna know where he came from because I might just join him on his nightly jogs. I don't know, but I'll see in the morning.

When the sun rose the next morning, I hear birds chirping and the warmth from the sun made me wake up with a smile. I finally got out of comfy my bed and headed to the kitchen where I am greeted with a fragrance that a hungry man would fall in love with. Thank God for my mother because she's the only person I know who would wake early enough to make sure we ate before we left and as usual my brother beat me to the table.

"Good morning," I say.

"Morning, Big Head," Trey says.

"Morning, Baby," my mother says.

"Are you excited about the tour of the school?" she asks.

"Yes ma'am, but what's for breakfast?" I ask. She starts to laugh and hands me my plate.

"So, what time you get off, Trey?" I ask him.

"Eight, I think. I gotta check when I get there."

My day is going to be super long with tours, filling out papers and going to get my State I.D.

"So, what time you think you'll be home Dee?" Trey asks me.

"Oh I don't know around three o'clock but I'm thinking about going for a jog when I get home and do a little writing," I tell him. After an hour of my morning writing, I finally went for a jog. I locked up the house up, did my warm-ups and officially started my day.

It's a nice day today for a jog, especially since I see this sexy figure coming towards me. When we finally got close to each other, I almost fainted because he is the same guy who I saw the other night jogging in the park behind the house. When we were just about to pass each other, I could've sworn I heard his sweet voice say, "Hi", so I spoke back. "OMG!" is all I could say. All I could do is turn around and stare at a gorgeous figure jog through these hot Cincinnati streets. Something in me told me to say more but I gotta make it to my school before it closes. I decide to call Julia and tell her about this cute new guy and tell her about Ryan.

"Hey, Bestie! How is Cincinnati Treating you so far?" she asks without saying hi.

"Julia, I have bigger fish to fry. I think I'm in love," I tell her.

"Oh, no! With who? Ain't it kinda too early for all this lovie dovie stuff? Demonte Durelle Bryant!"

"Did you just call me by my full government name?"

"And if I did?"

"I really can't stand you right now," I tell her as we both just laugh. "But look, I gotta go cause I'm close to the school," I tell her because I notice the jogger started to trail me.

"Ok but tell everybody said 'hi' especially yo sexy brother", she screams through the phone. For somebody that is so in love with my brother, she gets super shy around him.

He finally catches up to me and slow jogs in front of me but I notice that he's jogging towards the school. So, I try my best to keep up with him so I speed up and my suspicions were right; he goes to UC. He is wearing a nicely fitted UC shirt and UC sweatpants. I'm stuck in a daze the whole time I'm doing the paperwork for financial aid and planning my classes for the semester. After countless hours of school rules, expectations and taking a tour of the school I ran into the jogger. Right at that moment, I was lost for words; stuttering and all.

"Hey," I say, blushing and all.

"Hi," he says with the cutest dimples and prettiest white teeth.

"My name is Carlos. What's yours?"

Omg! No, he didn't just ask me for my name. Breathe Demonte, breath.

"It's Demonte."

"Oh, nice name," he says.

"Thanks. Your name is too!"

Okay, now things are just getting a little awkward between us.

"Um, I gotta go. I hope to see you some other time," I say. "Oh, yeah I'm so sorry. I gotta go too because I got a lecture in my next class this way."

We stared at each other's eyes and said our 'Good-Byes'. I so wish I coulda went with him, I swear I do. As I walked down the street I texted Briana telling her that I would be calling her and Christina later to give them my latest bombshell. I skipped happily down my street with the biggest smile on my face. I was so peaceful so I decided to go to the park to write until I received a phone call from a 'Restricted Number' so I ignored it. The number keeps calling and calling for fifteen minutes.

The number called again so I answered.

"Hello?" I answer.

All I heard was heavy breathing on the other end. "I'll get you my pretty," a strange voice answered before hanging up.

Okay, now this is so crazy. I really don't have time for the games but who cares because I see something I want. I finally get home to change my clothes for dinner but for some reason, I'm not in the mood for "A Family Night Out". I decided to call Julia to fill her in with the "Jogger" because I feel like I'm about to burst if I don't tell somebody.

"So you just now decided to call me back, right?" she asks.

"Sorry, it's just I've been really busy with unpacking and registering for school but I do miss you guys," I tell her.

"Spill the juice right now because I know it's some good stuff."

"Julia, it's nothing I promise you it's not. But if you insist, it involves a chocolate cutie", I say teasing her. "Have you guys talked, acknowledged each other or anything? Come on you gotta tell me the full story here."

I got to say, when it comes to my love life, I swear no one is more excited to know about it more than Julia. I guess that's why she's my best friend because she actually cares.

"Well, I don't have all the facts because we haven't talked yet. I saw him last night jogging but then we saw each other today on our way to the school. I can tell you that he loves jogging because that's all he does when I see him."

"I'm super jealous right now. You know what? We'll just trade; you come back to Birmingham and I'll go back to Cincinnati in your place." Just then I hear somebody coming which means I need to run in the bathroom to get ready for the day. "Look, Julia, I'll call you when I get in tonight cause the 'Battle of the Bathroom' is about to begin," I tell her. We say our good-byes and I ran for it.

"Hey, Dee," Trey says when I made it to the hallway. I could tell it was something with him cause his voice gets deeper and he gets moody.

"Hey, Trey. What's wrong?" I ask.

"Ugh, nothing just tired and need a nap for real. Did Mama change her mind about going out for dinner?" he asks. I can't believe he straight lying to me and then on top of that, he tried to change the change the subject.

"No, but Trey for real stop playing with me. What's wrong?" We stand there for a minute then he rolls his eyes and sighs.

"Look, Jessica is talking about leaving me after we talked about her moving up here and us getting our own spot." I could tell that he was hurt badly about it.

Jessica is his girlfriend who I never liked for real and I'm pretty sure she knows it. I'm mean every relationship has its ups and downs but this chick done took my brother through it.

"Well, let me start getting ready and we'll talk some more because I wanna talk to you about something anyway," I tell him. I think today is the day I'll tell my brother that I'm gay but I don't know if I should tell him now. My mother finally makes it home and we roll out to the restaurant.

"So, Demonte, how was registration today?" she asks in the car.

"It was great. It was long but I'm just glad it's over. How was your first day of work?" I ask her.

"It was ok. Had a few rude customers but for the most part, it was great."

"How about you, Trey?" she asks him. "It was ok I guess." It was downhill from there because it was silent from that point on. We finally made it to the restaurant and got seated.

"I finally feel okay now. How about you two?" my mother finally asks, breaking the ice.

"I gotta agree. I feel a whole lot better too. I just wish it didn't have to happen to us you know." Trey says.

When Trey and I were younger our father tormented me and him for years. He made me sell myself sexually for money every night while my mom worked third shift and beat my brother out of spite. Through it all and a seven-year age difference, it made our relationship stronger.

"Well, Boys, what doesn't kill you only make you not only stronger but wiser. I'm just glad we make you wiser."

I got to admit, it didn't make me wiser because I was in an abusive relationship for how long?

Trey finally started talking and it was our usual joking session which made me feel better because I was starting to get a little depressed. The night finally ended at the restaurant so we headed home and that's when my phone started to ring but I didn't recognize the number.

"Hello?" I answered.

"Hey, Dee, this Ryan. Can we talk please?"

Some people just can't take no for answer because I'm pretty sure I told him it was over and I didn't wanna talk about nothing with him.

"Look! I told I didn't want to talk to you and I didn't want to make any contact with you. So why keep calling?" I snapped.

"But I love ---"click.

I hung up before I could let him tell me another lie.

"Who was that?" my other asks.

"Oh, nobody. I think it's time to get my number changed because random numbers keep calling," I respond to her.

My brother gave me a look like 'I know something's up'. That's what I get for having a close relationship with my brother because he always knows when I'm lying and I hate that. When we finally make it home my brother barges into my room and sits at my desk.

"So really, who was that?" he asks.

"Ryan," I reply.

"What does he want?"

"I don't know. I didn't even give him a chance to explain why he called me."

"That's good cause I never liked him anyway. So, what you got planned for tomorrow?"

"Well I start school and I gotta put in this app at the library for this position that I might enjoy doing. After all that is done I'm coming home and do some poetry and I might go out for a jog."

"Okay, well I'll see you in the morning because I'm about to go crash," he says.

"Okay, good night."

"Good night."

I finally get dressed for bed and decided to text Briana to tell her to call me in the morning. The next morning, I get up and eat breakfast my mother made me before she left. She also left me a note saying that my aunt was supposed to be stopping by later to see us. I can't wait because this is the same aunt that I grew up around that I loved so much. I finally leave the house and head towards the school and it happened again; I ran into the jogger again.

"Hi", he says walking past me.

"Hey." I'm super nervous for no reason.

"Excuse me, but do you go to UC?" I ask trying to make a small conversation.

"Yeah, I do. Today's your first day?" he asks.
"Yeah, how can you tell?"

"Well I kind of saw you go into the 'Advisor's Office' the other today," he says. We walked quietly for about a block or two before I started the conversation back up.

"So, do you jog often?"

"Yeah. I jog at least four or five miles a day. Do you jog?"

"Yeah, I just haven't since we moved back here because I've super busy." Ok, I just lied big time. I don't jog and wasn't planning on to until just now. Ok, what's one little white lie?

"Would you like jog with me sometime this week when you're not 'busy'."

Bingo! Touchdown! Ok, Demonte, play it cool.

"Sure, that'll be great," I tell him. We finish the walk to the school in total silence, but I had the biggest smile on my face. "So what's your name again?" he finally asks.

"Demonte, Demonte Bryant. What's your name?"

"Carlos Johnson."

We finally make it to the school and I ask 'Can I text you sometime?'

"Um, sure?" We traded phones and saved numbers. I'm too excited now.

Chapter Three

No Where But Up

This morning went by quickly. It went by so quickly I don't remember getting ready for my first day. Now as I stand in front of the University of Cincinnati, it hits me that I have a fresh start in life away from Ryan and my father. It feels like a lot of weights have been lifted off my shoulders. Though it sometimes still feels as if somebody is still watching me, which makes the heavy burdens come back. I'll just shake it off because I only have a half hour before my first class and I still have to make it to the admissions office to get my schedule.

When I finally do get my schedule, it leaves me with ten minutes to get to "Business 101" which looks like it's all the way across campus. I walk in with three minutes to spare to a crowded room (well, almost crowded) with a somewhat young man sitting at the desk. This young man, who I'm guessing is Mr. Lee, looks like he is his early forties, with flawless chocolate skin, and stands about 6 foot 3 inches. When I first walked in, we made slight eye contact with a smile that has the prettiest white teeth a man could have but I stopped looking because he is the teacher and I am the student.

"Ok Class. Let's get started," he says, "I'm Mr. Lee and I will be teaching you 'Business 101.'"

'Wow' is all I can say because I swear he did it again. It was like he looked me straight in the eyes and smiled. I try to smile it off but I started feeling all warm inside. I try to focus on something else like actually taking notes.

"I'll be passing around the syllabus for this semester and please keep up with this one because I only give out one copy," Mr. Lee states.

"Well, this is going to be one rough course," I say to myself.

"Who you telling? I just hope I pass the math part of it," this chick says after my remark.

We both look at each other and laughed.

"My name is Julia. What's yours?" she asks.

"The name is Demonte."

"Is there something you two would like to share with the class?" Mr. Lee asks.

We both shake our heads 'no'.

"Well, please keep the talking down to a minimum in my class," he responds.

It's funny because, from the looks of it, Julia and I share the same exact schedule. After our morning schedule which was filled with 'Look to your left, look to your right' speeches, Julia and I went out for lunch.

"So, Demonte, are you from Cincinnati?" Julia asks.

"Yeah, but my family and I moved to Alabama when I was younger. What about you?"

"Well, no, I'm from Maysville, Kentucky. I always wanted to go to UC to get away from the small city life, you know."

"Oh, really? I just wanted to start over back in Cincinnati. After what I went through in my life, I just wanted to something different," I say looking away.

"So, what's on the menu for lunch today?" she asks.

"Oh, I don't know, pizza maybe."

When we get to the food court, I see this "Help Wanted" board by the door and I notice that the Public Library of Cincinnati and Hamilton County is hiring.

"I don't see anything interesting on here. You see anything?" she asks.

"Yeah, I think I do" I reply.

We went and got our food and found a table.

"That Mr. Lee is going to be a tough nut to crack," she says.

"Well, if you need any help, I'll help you," I say.

As we talk, I scan the sea of faces and for a second, I think I see Ryan's but just like that he was gone.

"What's wrong?" Julia asks.

"Oh, nothing. I just thought I saw somebody I didn't wanna see."

Just then I spot Carlos, and Julia spots me staring at him.

"Demonte, your hair is on fire," I think I hear her say.

"That sounds great. You should try it."

"Demonte, SNAP out of it!" she shouts.

We both start laughing, but I start blushing.

"You like him, don't you?"

"Yeah. Maybe and if I do?"

Why do I have to make it look so obvious that I'm attracted to a guy?

"Is it okay if I call him over?" I ask.

"Sure, go for it. Just know if something goes wrong, I had no part and I'm leaving," she says.

So, I get up and walk towards him with a walk a supermodel would be jealous of.

"Hey, Carlos."

"Hey, Demonte."

I feel my cheeks getting red all of a sudden.

"I was wondering if you'd like to eat lunch with me and my friend Julia?" I ask.

One thing people know about me is the fact that I hate rejection. I always have and I always will because I've always been the quiet version of my brother.

"Ugh, sure just let me grab my stuff and I'll be over there," Carlos says.

I run back to the table with the biggest smile on my face and from the look of my smile, Julia knows why.

"So, what did you say to him?" she asks.

"I asked him to come over and have lunch with us."

"You just asked him that? With a smile like that, I thought you asked dude out on a date."

Just then he starts to make his way towards our table.

"Girl, here he comes," I whisper to her.

"Hey everybody," he says sitting his stuff down.

"Hey," Julia replies.

"Carlos this Julia; Julia this is Carlos," I say.

They both shake hands.

"So, what's your major?" I ask Carlos.

"My major is Accounting with Business Management as my minor. What about you?" he responds.

"I'm also taking Business Management with Julia. So Julia, how do you like it so far here?" I ask trying to pull her into the conversation.

"I like it and I really think it is awesome here," she says giving me that, 'It's your moment' look.

"Look, I'm sorry to break this up but I just remembered that I'm supposed to meet some of my girls in the park," she says.

She grabs her stuff mouthing "Sorry".

"Well, I guess it's just the two of us, huh?" Carlos asks.

"I'm afraid so. So do you have any siblings?" I ask.

"Ugh, yeah. I have a little brother and an older sister. How about you?"

"I have an older brother. We are very close, I guess."

We sat there quietly or ten minutes staring at our trays.

"So, do you have a girlfriend by any chance?" I ask.

That was very straight forward and a little embarrassing. How do I manage to ask him that? That's really just setting me up for failure really.

"No, I don't. I'm really not looking at the moment," he replies.

Well, stop teasing me so much because you know your body is what I want.

"So, why did you choose accounting?" I ask.

"Well, to join my father at his accounting firm that's been passed down from his grandfather then to his father then my father and now to me. I'm a little excited but I feel like I wanna do something outside my family tradition," he says. "But enough about me, tell me a little bit about you."

"Well, my grandfather owns this chain of stores in Alabama that I really would love to take over one day. Running a business has always been one of my dreams coming up as a kid."

I feel really shy in front of him all of a sudden. We sat at the table for another ten minutes just in silence.

"So um, what types of sports do you like?" I ask.

"I'm a real versatile guy. I really do love football and basketball. How about you?"

"Same here, but I'm really into baseball."

"Really? My father and I used to always go to the opening day game and parade before he passed away from cancer," Carlos tells me.

"I'm so sorry to hear that. What kind of cancer did he have?"

"It's okay, really. He had liver cancer and the doctors said it was too late to treat it so it was like 'Where do we go from here?' situations.

I check my watch to see how much time I have before my next class starts and just my luck I got only ten minutes.

"I hate to cut this short but I gotta get to my next class. Is it okay if I text you later?" I ask him.

"Sure, I would like that."

We exchange numbers and I beeline it to my next class. On my way there, I swear I see Ryan but my eyes could be fooling me.

Chapter Four

The Dinner

Yesterday was such a blur that I barely remembered what went on but I do but I do remember rushing home to start on that application for the library. I finally crawl out of my nice warm bed to get breakfast started and to my surprise, I was home alone. I decided to text Briana to see what her plans were for today.

"Oh, nothing…did anything exciting happen yet?!?!?!?!?!? Give the details because I know something happened," she replies. So I decided to call and tell her about Carlos.

"So what's going on?" she asks without greeting me.

"Well, nothing really just school and looking for a job. I really don't have time for anything else. How are you?" I ask.

"School, working while trying to avoid your crazy ex and Brian. Ryan has called and texted me and he even came to my job looking for you. I'm telling you, dude got problems," she says.

She never liked Ryan because he was "no good". She's right because if you loved me the way he did, you wouldn't wanna hurt me.

"Sorry about that. What did he want with me?" I asked her.

"I ain't give him a chance to say nothing 'cause I called security on him."

We both started laughing. Julia is quick to call security on somebody when she don't feel like being bothered she calls the mall security and I think they've noticed.

"Well, look my break is almost up so I'll call you later. Bye," Julia says.

"Okay, bye."

With a whole day and nothing to do, I decided to go for a walk in the park with my notebook. I can't believe how beautiful Cincinnati is when the season change. Like the way the ice covers the tree branches or how the leaves are green and full of life or like now they are an assortment of different shades of fall colors. It helps me write better because it soothes me. While I was there, I saw little kids playing, elderly couples sitting on the benches, and an assortment of people jogging.

I finally get to the top of the park that has the view of Kentucky from Cincinnati. I decide to grab a bench to write some poetry while I watch the view. For the longest time, I felt like I was okay and I never went through anything as foul as I did. I felt nature taking over my body while restoring my soul. Before I knew it, I wrote at least three pages and my hand is starting to hurt. I sat there a little longer to finish watching the view when I hear a familiar speak to me.

"So, this is what you do with your free time, huh?"

I turn around to see that it is Carlos.

"Hello to you too, stranger," I respond. We fist bump while he jogged in place. I don't know why we keep running but I kind of like it.

"So, you here writing that next hit poem?" he asks sarcastically.

"Well, yes I am. What are you here besides jogging?" I ask.

Clearly, he is here to simply to jog through the park.

"Just checking out the sights and relieving some stress. It's good to just let it go because it's unhealthy to keep it in. How do you relieve your stress?" he asks.

"That's a good question. I guess through writing and the occasional jog I take. I'm a huge fan of writing poetry because I can express my feelings through rhyming. But then there is jogging. I could just sweat it out and somewhat run from it," I tell him

"We should go got a jog sometime, but I gotta go, okay?"

"Oh, yeah, go right ahead. See you later," I say.

"See you around," he says jogging away.

I keep writing for at least another hour. On my way home my phone keeps vibrating and I check the screen to see a phone call from Ryan. I ignore it of course but he keeps calling so I turn my cell phone off. When I finally get home my mom, brother, and to my surprise, my aunt is there.

"Hey, Aunt Terry," I say as I walk in the door.

"Hey, Baby. Boy, you and your brother are really growing up so fast," she says while giving me a hug and a kiss.

I shoot my brother a 'What is she doing here?' look and we both start laughing. Don't get me wrong, we love our aunt but there is just something about her that hint that she just a two face person. I mean she Treated us like her own as kids but I just more pieces to the puzzle.

"I miss you two so much and I was so happy to hear that you guys were moving back up here that it became my main conversation piece with everyone I talked to. But Demonte I hear that you and your education decision is the reason why everybody came back home," my aunt says.

"Ugh, yeah. I really wanted to get my degree in Accounting and Business Management but it wouldn't mean as much if I didn't get it from The University of Cincinnati," I tell her.

I just wish she would stop faking it and keep it real. See, my aunt has this law firm where she is the founding partner and she feels as she is the best at what she does but I feel as if she thinks she is God Almighty. I just pray that this night goes by smoothly because a horrible family dinner is the last thing I need to worry about. From the aroma from the kitchen, I can tell my mom is making her famous cornbread and oven barbequed chicken.

"So, I hear that you have an interview at the library coming up. Are you nervous?" my aunt asks me.

"Um, not really. I feel like I'll get the job especially with all of the interview training I went through in high school."

"That's great honey. I'm praying that you get the job and that it benefits you well."

Just then my mom finally comes out of the kitchen to join us in the living room around the television.

"So, what are we watching?" my mom asks.

"Double Jeopardy," my brother says. The only reason why he knows is because it's his all-time favorite movie other than Man on Fire.

"Well look, dinners ready all we have to do is set the table and wash our hands. Demonte, can you help me with the table?"

"Oh, no, Joy. I'll help you set the table," my aunt says following my mother to the kitchen.

So, now my brother and I are heading to the bathroom and I feel as if I should tell him now that I'm gay but I'm afraid of how he would react to the thought of his little brother being a homosexual. I can't lie; just the thought of him physically attacking me scares the living hell out of me. I have read blogs about how different guys family members have jumped them, turned their backs on them and even have publicly humiliated them as a person spreading their personal business out.

"What should I do?" is going through my mind. Why am I so nervous to ask him out to lunch to tell him something that is so important to me? I promise you that I love my brother but it's so hard me mentally that it's affecting me in the worse way. Am I a bad little brother for being gay?

"So, ugh do you wanna go out for lunch tomorrow? My treat?" I ask.

"Oh, boy. What's wrong?"

Busted! Why do I always show that I'm nervous, scared, or mad about something? I am not too good at not showing my emotions.

"Nothing's wrong. I just want to spend some time with my big brother that's all."

"Naw buddy, I know better when it comes to you. What's going on with you?"

"Boys, what's taking so long?" my mother calls from downstairs.

"Ugh, look we'll talk about it tomorrow," I say drying my hands.

I just want to honest with the two people I love the most, but I don't wanna hurt them either. I ran out of the bathroom and down the steps making sure that I didn't give him a chance to pressure me anymore.

"So Demonte, I hear that you are attending the University of Cincinnati in Blue Ash. What's your major?" my aunt asks.

"Yes, ma'am. I'm majoring in Business Management with Accounting as my minor. Are you still at that big-time law firm?" I ask.

I really could care less, just like she cares less about what school I'm attending or major. Do you see where I'm going with this? I'm not trying to be one of those disrespectful hoodlums that have no purpose in life. I really love my aunt but I'm tired of faking it to make it around her.

"Oh no. I quit that firm and started my own firm. You and Trey should someday come down to start your career in the law department. I'm right downtown on Race Street," she tells us.

She is some big league criminal lawyer and pretty good at it. She is known all over the United States, like Johnny Cochran. I wish I had a better relationship with her because I need a second mother like female in my life.

"That'll be great! That way you could spend quality time with your aunt. So did you take your receptionist with you?" my mother asks.

Let's not talk about him because we all knew was gay by the way he acted.

"Who, Greg? No, he died back when I first left the firm from a car accident on a suicide mission," she tells us.

"I'm so sorry to hear that. I just don't understand why somebody would want to take their own life. Do you know what was going on with him personally?"

"No, but it was word going around that he was being bullied because of his sexuality from his family, friends and complete strangers. I think it's true because I remember him coming to the office with a black eye. Of course I asked him about it but he keeps avoiding the question with 'I'm okay. I just had too much to drink last night' kind of answer."

"That's just sad that he went through that," my mother comments.

Things kind of got awkwardly quite while we finally started eating.

"So Trey, how was your day?" I ask him.

"It was cool. We had it easy today because the mall was shut down because the stores begged the mall owners to close early for some big inventory count. So fewer people, less drama," he responds.

So after that, it was down Memory Lane from there. Mom told Aunt Terry some embarrassing stories about us when we were growing up in Birmingham; half of them we remembered and some we didn't. We finally finished dinner heading on over to dessert and got Mom's favorite movie started, The Phantom of the Opera. We laughed, cried and then we got mad on some parts. After the movie, we started cleaning up and got my aunt ready to go giving her a hug.

"Good night everybody," she says as we watch her walk to her car.

While Trey and Mama were watching the news, I beeline it to the bathroom to hop in the shower. While I'm in the shower, I hear my phone constantly going off but I ignore it until my mother yells at me to turn it off. When I got to my room to check it, I see that I got five missed calls from Ryan. I politely go to his contact info and block him. After I got fully dressed, I grabbed my poetry book and went to the back porch to write. With my headphones blaring out smooth jazz, I didn't notice my brother come out.

"Hey, you cool?" he asks tapping me on my shoulder.

"Yeah, I'm cool. Why you ask?"

"The only time you come outside in your pajama is when you're stressed out. So what's going on?' he continues to ask.

"I just want everything with me, school and trying to get my career as a writer started that's all. You of off all people should know how important my poetry is to me," I tell him hoping he would take that as my excuse.

"Okay, but if you ever need to talk to you know where to find me," he says walking towards the door.

I really hate hiding stuff from my brother but I don't know how to tell him that his only little brother is gay. But I do know that I don't wanna be like my aunt's assistant who killed himself because of his sexuality. After being outside enjoying the fall breeze and watching the stars I finally make my way to my bed and text Brianna, Bryant and Christina 'Good Night'. I woke up the next morning late as usual after a night of tossing and turning. I skipped out on breakfast and mad a dash to school. During my rush of a morning, I notice a text from Carlos saying "Good morning Buddy!!!" I replied with "Good Morning, You..." Then that's when I received a phone call from the library about an interview sometime next week. It's really looking good for me. I ran to my first to class hoping I got there extra early to make sure I grabbed a seat by Julia.

"You almost lost your seat. Why you so late?" she asks.

"Good morning to you, too. I woke up late this morning because I didn't get any good sleep last night," I tell her.

"Oh, you okay?"

"Yeah, I'm perfectly fine. Why you ask?"

"Well, that's usually people tend to toss and turn. Either that or you got an old mattress," she tells me.

I really didn't wanna go into details with her before class start nor did I want to tell her because I barely know her for real. Call me shy but I just don't feel comfortable with telling her what was going on at home. I do figure that the surprise visit from Aunt Tracey and the talk about her assistant did make me feel kind of confused and uncomfortable down in my soul.

That's why I had to write outside last night to try and get some type of comfort. Class starts five minutes after I get there but it's kinda hard to focus when you have a cutie like Carlos texting you. He asks me about my morning and my plans. I also told him about my interview which he is happy to hear about it. The conversation was so good that Julia had to snap me out of my phone.

"What I miss?" I ask as I snap out of my daze.

"The whole lecture and the part about us having a paper due next week,' she tells me.

"Where was I at when this paper came up?" I ask her.

Just then, Mr. Lee shots us a look that sent chills through me. I can tell that Julia caught it too cause she started looking down at her book. I secretly sent Jessica a message saying 'What's his problem?!' She looked at me and giggled. The last fifteen minutes of class went by real quick and while I trying to make a quick exit but Mr. Lee still managed to catch me.

"Mr. Bryant, may I have a word with you please?" he asks in a very demanding voice.

I shot Julia a look and she nods at me, walking out the door with the rest of the class. I'm not go lie but I'm super nervous. When Mr. Lee goes to close, I can see Julia lingering around the door like a trooper.

"First day here and you strike up a conversation during the middle of my lecture, but then further it with texting. What is it? Are you bored with my class? If you are, I advise you to drop my class while you have a chance. There are a lot of intelligent, young minds out there that are willing to take my class," he says.

"But Mr. Le…" I start to say.

"But, nothing. I see too much potential in you, which is why it'll be too hard for me to fail you. But if you don't get your act together, I'll have to drop you as a student," he says as he opens the door. "Good day, Mr. Bryant."

I politely walked out of the class without uttering a word.

"So, what he say?" Julia asks before I could walk out of the door good.

"I need to calm down the talking or he'll drop me off of his roster."

"Bummer," she replies.

The day was moving at a moderate rate which didn't matter to me cause all it I could do is think about Carlos. My phone vibrates letting me know that I have a text from Trey.

"Momma said she's working a double so we on our own with dinner... Wanna go out for dinner?" he sends.

"Yeah, that's cool...," I reply.

I'm in my accounting class, zoned out and thinking about Carlos and my brother. In a way, I want to introduce Carlos to Trey but Trey still doesn't know that I'm gay. I really have to tell him about it and I might just tell him over dinner. I might meet up with Julia at our usual spot so I could tell her about tonight. I took a nice little walk home admiring natures beauty thinking about tonight.

I just want to be honest with my family about what's going on in my life because I'm tired of hiding it. When I get home, I check the mailbox and while I look over I catch a shirtless Carlos with a smile. The more I think and see Carlos, the more eager I get to tell my family. I know I've only known Carlos for a couple months but I really see myself with him in a serious relationship. We speak to each other before I ran into the house to get ready to go out for dinner. My brother is already home already as usual.

"What's up bra?" my brother says.

"I'm good. What's up with you?" I ask.

"Nothing much, just waiting on you. I'm ready whenever you are," he tells me.

"Aight." I jet to my room with my cell phone in hand hoping to get a text from Carlos.

I send Brianna a text saying, 'Today is the day I tell my brother my secret!!!! ☐ :-(Wish me luck!!! TTYL, D'.

"OMG!!!! Let me know what he says!!!! I'm so happy 4 u!!!!"

I fix myself up and meet my brother outside by the car.

"How is school going for you?" he asks me when I get in the car.

"It's going good. Just one of my professors giving me a hard time," I tell him.

I'm really starting to feel like a little kid running to his older brother whining.

"D, just keep it easy, cause we both know how you live to talk. So chill," he warns me.

I turn my head and rolled my eyes.

"Man aight. How's work going for you?" I ask.

"It's good. I'm about to get a raise and a promotion and a raise but don't go running telling mama," he tells me.

"I won't, but I'm happy for you."

We finally get to the restaurant and get seated. When we sat down, we started watching the game, laughing and talking enjoying each other's company. Tonight, I finally can say I see a different side of him that makes me feel comfortable in telling him that I'm gay. We ordered wings for appetizers and a large meat lovers pizza with extra meat.

"So, I got a question," I say to him.

"I got an answer," he replies.

I really am struggling to come up with the words to tell him but I don't know why. He looks at me like he wants to say 'What's the question?'.

"How do you feel about lesbians and homosexuals?" I ask him.

"I ain't got nothing against them just come at me with it. Why?" he asks.

"Just asking because a couple people at school I know came out. They said that the people flipped on them and even kicked them out of their house."

I have the perfect chance to tell him that I'm gay but I don't know why it won't come out. We finally grab the check and to my surprise, my brother pays. We get in the car full of silence with nothing to say. I felt a spark of courage but I started fighting it but I couldn't hold it in.

"I'M GAY!" I shout out.

He keeps driving looking forward as if he didn't hear me.

"Did you hear me?" I ask.

Then I see his veins pop out if his forehead which means he is either hurt or mad.

"Yeah, I heard you but I think that I misunderstood what you said. Did you just say that you're gay?"

All of a sudden I feel my face getting warm and it hits me that I'm crying to myself. We get home and he runs, with me on his heels, to his room slamming the door to his room in my face.

"TREY! Please, can we just talk! Please!"

He just ignores my plea of reconciling. The feeling of being disconnected from my brother finally hits me like a ton of bricks. I go to my room, still fully dressed, to cry myself to sleep. I promise that I never felt this about anything in my life. All I know is I can't and will not make it without my brother.

Chapter Five

The First Date

Today is the day I get to start over. Today is the day I have my interview with the library. I hope I get the job even with the way the conversation I had with my brother ended is still bothering me. Ever since then we've been out of sync so bad to the point my mother even noticed.

"What's the matter with you two? I haven't seen you two hold a conversation all week," she asks.

"Ask him," he says shrugging his shoulders walking away.

WOW! 'Ask him' though. I just got up and got ready for my interview.

"Hey, Dee. So what happened?" Brianna asks as soon as she answered the phone.

"Well, we are not talking right now. You, out of all people know how bad this is killing me. I can't go minutes without talking to him. So imagine how a whole week is making me feel," I tell her with tears rolling down my face.

"Dee, it's going to be okay. He's just hurting right now because he just found out his little brother is gay. He's just probably having a hard time processing it. Just give him time; he'll come around because he loves you."

Deep down inside I know this but my mind won't wrap around that.

"I know, but what I do know is I'm getting this job no matter what is going on in my life," I tell her.

"I know it's hard for you, but you gotta give him time to process it. But look, call me later cause I gotta get ready for work," she says.

"Ok, talk to you later," I say hanging up.

All I could do is sit there and cry. I finally pull it together and head to my interview. When I finally get to the library, I notice that I'm thirty minutes early which gives me more than enough time to find the right department.

"Hi, my name is Demonte and I'm here for a one o'clock interview with Ms. Gina Watkins," I say to the lady at the department desk. She looks at the computer screen then her notepad.

"Okay, Demonte, have a seat over there in our waiting area. My name is Alice and I'll let Gina know you are here bright and early," she says.

From what I can see, she has a cocoa caramel complexion going on with a natural hairstyle. From the way she's sitting, she looks like she could be more than five foot six inches. I see her leave the desk and head to the back which I'm hoping to get Gina. I text Brianna saying,

'I'm super nervous!!!!!! Pray 4 me PLZ!!!!'

For some reason, I get this cold chill, which makes me feel unsure about the job. Around 12:50 this six foot, even early 30's, looking woman comes out of the door Allice went through and stops at the desk. I guess she was looking for me because they both looked and pointed towards me.

"Demonte?" she asks when she got close enough.

I stand up and greet her with a nod, ready to shake hands.

"Hey! My name is Gina and I'm the department manager. I'll also be giving you an interview and a shelving test. Are you ready?"

"Yes, Ma'am I am."

I whisper a prayer the whole way to the table and with every step the feeling got worse.

"So, Demonte, tell me a little bit about yourself," she starts with.

"Well, I was born in Cincinnati and raised in Birmingham. My and I recently moved back to Cincinnati so I could attend the University of Cincinnati. I'm a hard working young adult with an 'I'm here to work' mentality. I'm very dependable and will get the job done at a steady rate that not will not only please you but the entire library staff," I start telling her.

My mother taught me to always take over the interview to make sure I get the job.

"So, what do you think you could bring to the library to better us as an organization?" she asks me.

"I could better the library with my people skills. I love helping people especially when it could better their selves. With this job I feel like I'm giving back to humanity and to my community," I tell her trying to sound like I was trying to kiss up already.

I really could use the money so it won't look like I'm not trying to help out around the house financially. While Gina started telling me the expectations of the library, I get sidetracked by this little cute young buck. I ain't go lie, I was checking him out. From what I can see from my seat is the fact that he has a Hershey chocolate complexion and standing about five foot ten. While I 'm checking him out, I kind of chime back in on Gina's little speech about the library.

"So, with that being said, do you think you can handle the job?" she asks.

"Yes Ma'am, I sure am."

I totally do not know what I agreed to, but I know he is fine.

"Ok, well, Demonte, we're done with the interview. Do you have any questions for me?" she asks.

"How soon will I know if I got the job?"

"I should know by tonight but I'm not making any promises. So excuse me while I go talk to the rest of the board members," she says as she smiles and walked away.

My fingers are crossed together so tight that I start losing feeling in them. I call Carlos to tell him the good news but it goes to voicemail. Before I could get a chance to call him back, he calls me.

"Hey, you. Sorry I missed your call but when I went to go answer, you went to voicemail," he tells me.

"It's okay. I completely understand. I was just calling you to tell you that I'm runner up for the job," I tell him.

"Congratulations! I'm so happy for you, I really am. What are you doing tonight?" he asks.

"Ugh, I really don't know."

I'm so hoping he asks me out because this would put the icing on the cake.

"Well, I was just wondering if you'd like to go out for dinner and a movie, maybe?"

BINGO! For a moment I got tongue-tied.

"Demonte you still there?"

"Yeah, I'm still here."

"Is it too soon, because if it is, I'm sorry. I just wanna go out as friends," he says.

"No, no your fine. I'd really like that," I reassure him.

"Great! How about if I meet you at your house around seven?"

"That'll be perfect. Ok, it's official then. I'll catch you later."

"Later!"

I did my "I did that" dance right in the middle of the department. That boy doesn't know how much he made my day. I wonder if he wants to take it further than 'just friends' because I know I do. I'm trying to play it cool but I wanna leap for joy. To be honest, I really haven't been on a date since Ryan. We rarely went anywhere as a couple because he always thought I was checking out other guys. Or he didn't like me being around Bryant because he knew how Bryant really felt about me. I do wonder how things would be if I had chosen Bryant over Ryan. Mr. Cutie burst me out of my train of thought when I bumped into him knocking the books out of his hands.

"I'm so, so sorry. Let me help you out," I'm telling him bending picking up books.

"It's fine because I wasn't paying attention," he says to me.

I help tuck the books back into his arms. He smells and even looks better up close.

"My name is Craig. I see that you had an interview earlier. What's your name?" he asks.

"The name is Demonte, Demonte Bryant," I say as we shake hands.

We stand here in silence, blushing and doing cute little laughs.

"Um, I gotta go. It was nice meeting you," I say before walking away.

"Yeah, me too. Nice meeting you as well," he says.

We both walk away with a smile on our faces. I feel like Stella like I got my groove back. What really got me going is the date I have with Carlos later. I wonder where we are going because I'm pretty sure Carlos will not tell me but then again it'll probably be somewhere long and romantic. The ride home from the interview was until I got home and ran into Carlos.

"Hey, you! Are you ready for tonight?" he greets me with.

"Hey there yourself. It depends; have you been a good little boy today?" I say giving him a sheepish smile running in the house.

On my way in, I notice that my brother car is parked out front but the house is quite as ever. Ma probably dropped him off at work to save on gas which was fine with me. I dropped my stuff in the living room running straight into my room.

"TREY!" I shout as I walk into my room seeing him sitting on the edge of my bed all nonchalantly.

"What are you doing in my room?"

"I need to talk to you. We both need to talk about you being 'gay'," he says choking on every word.

"Ok. What do wanna know?" I ask.

I start shaking not knowing what to expect. I do know for a fact that he's hurt because his eyes are lighter. For some reason our eye color always changes with our mood; the lighter they are the more hurt we are but the darker the madder.

"Why, just why, this route?" he asks.

We just sat there in quietness for a while staring at each other. I never really knew why I was gay and I definitely didn't wanna give him the whole "I was born this way" speech.

"I wish I could tell you but I don't fully understand myself. I just know that I'm not the average little brother you wanted me to be," I tell him.

Before I know it, I just start crying. Tears just started pouring out of me and I felt arms wrapping around me. We both are crying at this point which made me feel a whole lot better. That told me that he felt my pain.

"Just know I still love you and you are still my little brother, no matter what. I'm just happy that you told me and nobody else. But why are you just now telling me?"

"I don't know. I guess always felt like you would disown me as your blood brother. I still haven't told Mama."

"In due time. But look, I gotta get ready for this dinner date with a friend from school," I tell him.

"Just know this conversation ain't over," he says leaving my room.

He just never gives anything up because as far as I'm concerned, it is. Getting ready is a breeze but before I knew it, Carlos was ready and calling.

"Okay, okay. I'm on my way out now," I tell him.

He meets me at the end of my walkway like a real gentleman. On my way towards him, I notice something in his hand.

"For you," he says handing me a single red rose.

"Aww, thank you! This is so sweet of you," I say giving him a hug.

"So, are you ready for a romantic night?" he asks

"Yeah, but where are we going?"

"You'll see," he tells me with a grin on his face.

We started walking towards the park where I see a picnic set up complete with a candle lit, a blanket and another rose by a Trey.

"Do you like?" he asks.

"It's beautiful. I especially like how you got it set up by the view, but why here?" I ask.

"I know because if you are just now telling me, I know you ain't tell Mama

"You seem very relaxed here. I didn't want you all tensed up while we are on our date."

We both have a seat on the blanket where a 2-liter of Pepsi, two cups and a bucket of ice was waiting on us.

"So, why are you always so tense?" he asks staring me in my eyes.

"I'm not tense. I just have a lot on my mind that makes me look tense," I respond.

"Well, what do you think about?"

I tried to pass the question for a second with him staring at me.

I really don't feel like I can trust him yet so I lie and say "Life".

"Oh, well, does your family know that you are gay?" he asks.

"What's up with all the low blow questions?" I wanna scream.

"My brother and I were just talking about it while I was getting dressed and my mot-," I pause.

"Can you pass the chips?" I ask.

We sit there quiet not saying a mumbling word.

"So, uh, do you like your class schedule so far?" he finally asks.

"Yeah, it's getting better by the day. It's easy because my grandfather taught me everything about running a business. What about you?"

My phone vibrates letting me know that somebody is calling me but I ignore it. But then the caller texts me saying;

"I see it doesn't take long to replace me… Y'all do look happy… SIKE!!!"

I know now that I wasn't tripping. I start looking around hoping I see him but all I see is darkness.

"Is everything okay?" Carlos asks me.

"Ugh, yeah I'm just a little chilly."

Then he wraps his arm around me while we stare off into space. I finally feel like I can be vulnerable around somebody than my girls.

Chapter Six

The First Jog

So, I finally started training as a shelver which I was so excited about last week. Everybody here, including the patrons, are nice to me.

"So Demonte, do you like to anything outside of work and school?" Alice asks me.

"Well, I love writing poetry, short stories and music. Writing to me is my way of venting to the world and it really helps," I tell her.

"Oh, really, what is your book about?"

"I really don't know yet cause I'm still working out the outline for it. But I'm stuck between the life of a preacher's kid or a good murder mystery."

I really don't like talking about my writing because I'm shy, scared of rejection and people stealing my ideas.

"Oh, sounds interesting. Are you trying to get published?" she asks.

"I really haven't thought about getting published," I tell her.

Just then, I see Gina coming towards the desk.

"Hey, Demonte, how are you today?" Gina asks with the prettiest white smile.

"Hey Ms. Gina, I'm great and you?" I respond.

"I'm fine, thank you. How's it going with your shelving skills come along?"

"I'm starting to get better by the day."

Just then, Craig walks out from the back. All week long we've been eyeing each other. I'll admit he is fine but it's something about him that reminds me of Ryan but that doesn't stop me from flirting with him, but he always starts the games.

"Demonte, can you shelve those books in the back by my office for me please?" Gina asks.

"Yeah, sure," I respond.

On my way to the back, I run into Craig of all people.

"Hey, Demonte, how are you today?" he asks me.

"I'm great, how about you?" I reply.

"I'm just a little tired."

We stand in the back awkwardly quietly because I'm shy and he has something to ask but doesn't know how to ask.

"Where are you from again?" he finally asks.

"I'm from Birmingham but you moved there from Cincinnati when I was younger. Have you been in Cincinnati your whole life?"

"Yeah. I've lived in the same house in Forest Park my whole life," he says with pride while looking in my eyes.

We stare into each other's eyes and I can tell that he's up to something or has a question to ask.

"Look, I gotta run these up front but I'll talk to you later," I say backing up into the door.

I quickly turn around because I can feel my cheeks turning red but he has a huge smile on his face. I begin shelving the books knowing he was watching but who cares right? Stashed in a corner typing a text to Carlos saying 'Can't wait to see you… Maybe a movie after?' After what felt like forever, I finally receive a text. 'Sounds great with dinner afterward… My Treat ☐!' 'Bet!'

Time seems to be moving a little slow since that conversation went down.

"Hey, Demonte you can go when you get down," Gina says, "cause I know you got something planned after work."

"How'd you know?" I ask.

She walks from behind the cubical with a beautiful bouquet of roses handing them to me.

"Sorry for being noisy, but they say 'Can't wait for tonight's run. Meet you at your place when you get off, Carlos.' So you wanna go or not?" I grabbed my stuff, gave her a hug and ran outta there with the flowers in my arm. The drive seemed endless because of my excitement to see Carlos. When I finally do pull up I see him and his mother taking groceries in the house so I ran to help.

"Well look who it is?" he says with the biggest smile on his face.

"Hey, Ms. Linda," I say, grabbing bags.

"Hey, there Baby," she says giving me a kiss on the cheek. Just put those bags by the kitchen sink. Carlos, why can't you find more friends like Demonte?"

We just look at each other smiling. We bee-lined it from the car to the kitchen with the groceries.

"So, do you wanna go for that jog?" he asks while walking me to the door. "Yeah I just gotta go change," I say, "Oh and the roses are beautiful. Thank you."

"You're welcome," he says blushing.

"But what's the occasion?"

"Oh, nothing I just wanted to do something nice for a change. So speaking of 'change', when are you going to change?" he asks laughing.

I roll my eyes walking away, "Okay, I'm leaving since somebodies in a big rush. I'll be back in 20 minutes."

I make a mad dash it to the door to meet my brother who I didn't hear nor see pull up.

"Well look who it is", he greets me with.

"What's good homie?" I ask giving him the fist bump.

"What you about to get into with your new friend?" he asks.

"What makes you think we got something planned?" I ask getting nervous.

Well, see I still haven't told my family that I was gay so any little thing sparks a suspicion that they know that I'm gay.

"Oh, I don't know. The way you didn't even notice that I pulled up or the fact that you had a huge smile on your face when you walked over here."

We finally make into the house which gave me the perfect opportunity to make a mad dash it to my room. I get to my room to change but instead, I find my brother following me.

"So, you ain't go tell me?" he asks me.

"We don't have nothing planned but a run through the neighborhood. Is it against the law or something?" I ask jokingly staring at him.

Only if looks could kill the look my brother is giving me would've been killed me.

"No it ain't, it's just I want you to be careful, okay?"

"Why wouldn't I be?" I ask.

Without answering my question, he just walks off. For a second, it sounded like my brother was pleading with me to be safe when I was around Carlos, but why? I pulled my phone and shot Briana and Christina a text saying, 'OMG!!! Y'all husband is straight tripping... I'll call y'all later and give details.' I grabbed my wallet and keys running towards the door to be greeted by Carlos.

"Somebody is a little impatient I see," I say with a smile.

"No, I just um, well um," he says, "I just wanted to make sure we didn't miss the movie."

"Well, what are we waiting for?" I say running past him playfully.

At first, we were just running not saying a word to each other but he would glance over at me smiling. I don't know where to go from here with him because a man including Ryan has ever made me feel this way. I fell as if I can finally be myself without being scared of getting rejected.

"So, how's school coming along?" he asks finally breaking the silence.

"It's coming along great. I got a presentation, three papers and a test due by next week which I'm almost done with," I say.

"I'm impressed."

We are coming close to the dead end of the street so we slowed done to take a break. I turn around to head back to the house but then Carlos grabs my arm pulling me back towards him.

"Hey, you're forgetting something," he says giving me the sincerest, longest kiss.

For a second, it feels like the world stopped and my heart dropped to the ground. I stop and look him dead in his eyes.

"What, did I do something wrong?" he asks. "I'm sorry I just uh."

"There's no need to be sorry it's just I'm not ready."

"I'm sorry. Let's get back to the house," he says.

If I thought the first part of the run was awkwardly quiet the run back was worse. I didn't mean to scare him away its just I'm still trying to get over Ryan. Carlos is a great guy but I just don't wanna rush into anything. When we finally get near the house I could see an extra car in the driveway which could only mean that my aunts there.

"So, are we still on for the dinner and a movie tonight?" he asks when we get to his driveway.

"Um, yeah I just gotta go change and see why my aunt here."

I get to the door to unlock it but it's already unlocked.

"Anybody home?" I call out.

"In the kitchen honey. Come say hi to your aunt," my mother responds.

It took everything for me to not to just go straight to my room but I went in anyway.

"Hey Aunt Terry," I say giving her a kiss and a hug.

"Hey Baby. Looks like somebody has been working out," she says.

"Yes, ma'am. Did a three-mile run and now I'm about to take a shower and head to the movies with a friend."

I just then feel a smile creep across my face with my checks turning red so I look away. I can't believe he got me feeling like this.

"Sounds like a date to me Joy," my aunt says.

"So, who's the lucky girl?" my mother asks.

"NO, it's not a date, it's just me and Carlos going out as homies, friends, amigos."

"Ok you sure?" my mother asks.

"Yes, ma'am I'm sure. Look ladies excuse me, I gotta go and get ready before I get left."

I run to my room as fast as I can because I know where that conversation was headed and I wasn't going like the outcome of it.

Chapter Seven

Breaking Out Of My Shell

What a night Carlos and I had! We went to go see a movie, went out to eat and for a walk in the park. For once I had somebody who actually wanted to listen to my story without passing judgment.

"I finally see why your brother is so overprotective," Carlos tells me.

We approach a bench under a beautiful purple tree. He reaches out for my hand which I'm hesitant to grab but I do it anyway.

"I have a confession to make but I don't know how to tell you," he says looking at me.

"What? Tell me," I say a little worried that he might not want to see me anymore.

"Well, um, well I have feelings for you and I want to be that man that makes you happy as your boyfriend. I wanna be your lover, your best friend," he says.

Things got quiet after he said that. We just sat there for the longest just looking into the view of the Kentucky state line.

"The other day when I kissed you, I really wanted to tell you then but I didn't know what to say."

"Well, you know my dilemma, I'm not ready. I know you're a great guy but I need to know that you're not going to hurt me like he did."

He grabbed me by my chin and laid a nice heavy kiss on me which I'm glad he is. He pulls away, eyes wide staring my soul down.

"Well, you are just gonna have to prove to me that I can trust and love you because I can't have my heart broken again," I tell him trying to fight back tears.

"Demonte, no relationship is perfect but I can try and promise not to hurt you. We are going to argue and fight, but I promise you that I love and care about you. Just give me a chance to try," he pleads.

By now we're standing up looking into each other's eyes with a single tear coming down. We were looking at each other as we were able to fix the problem that was bothering the other one's soul. I don't know what to do because my feelings are clouding my better judgment and I know this now. I just wish I could talk about to my brother.

"Look, it's getting late and I know you got school so let me get you home," he tells me. I nod my head and went to the car behind him.

When we finally get to the house and he walks me to the door like the perfect gentleman. I promise you I'm not going to look in his direction because he makes my emotions go crazy because really, I do love him but I can hide nothing from him. We finally get to my door and we turn to each other to say "Good Night" but instead he hit me with the longest, firmest kiss I ever got in my life.

"Demonte M Bryant, I'm in LOVE with you and I'll do whatever to prove to you that I do," he tells me.

"I love you too but-," I start to say before getting hushed.

"Look, just think about it and call me tomorrow," he says walking backward towards his house.

I stand here, even more confuse, because I wanna be with him but a part of me just wanna leave him alone because I don't wanna hurt him. I turn around to unlock the door and to my surprise, I walk in to see my mother just now going to bed.

"Hey Ma, you up late. You ok?"

"Yeah, I was just praying that you were okay. Next time you out this late, just call. Good Night," she warns me.

"Good night," I tell her before she closes her door.

I go to my room to get my night clothes before I feel my phone vibrates. Just my luck it's a message from Ryan saying, 'Demonte please talk to me I miss you… I love you!!!' A rush of hurt came over me and I just lost it until I fell asleep. I roll over to turn my alarm off, sore and all. Thanks to Ryan I sleep the wrong way, I didn't take a shower nor did I hear my alarm for 45 minutes late.

I got up and ran around my room gathering clothes running to the bathroom. On my way there I run into my ignorant brother.

"Look, who finally decides to come home after pulling an all-nighter," he says with a smirk.

I stop and look at him confused then I remember I didn't change.

"Morning to you too, Jerk. Actually, I got in while Mom was on her way to bed, thanks very much," I say with a huge grin.

"Ain't you running late for class anyway," he asks.

"Yeah, I'm debating if I even wanna go still."

"Li'l dude you going to school. Now act stupid and not go if you want to," he says with authority.

I just ran into the not even putting up a fight.

"That's what I thought little boy," I hear him say through the door.

I get through the rest of my early morning routine at home with ease. When I finally get to school I scan the grounds for Julia and when I see her under the big oak tree I run towards her with the biggest smile on my face.

"Good morning there," I greet her with when I get close.

"Morning. What's that big smile, though?" she asks.

"Well ugh, Carlos and I went out on a date last night. Let's just say things got emotional." I tell her.

She looks at me with excitement but then her facial expression change to confusion.

"What? What's wrong?" I ask.

"What's wrong is you? What did you do to him?" she asks.

"I didn't do anything. I just kinda didn't know what to because I'm still getting over Ryan."

"Ok, I forgive you… this time." We both start giggling like little kids.

Just then Carlos walks by with a group of friends and spots me on the lawn. He says something to them and comes my way with an even bigger smile, which causes me to start blushing. Julia notices this and looks at me laughing and starts to get up.

"Where are you doing?" I ask getting up with her.

"Hey, you. I called you this morning but you picked up then hung up on me," he asks.

I start to check myself and bag for my phone to realize I don't have my phone.

"That's crazy because I think I forgot it at home, sorry." I start to blush even harder.

"You remember Julia right?" I ask.

"Yeah. Hey, how are you?" he asks.

"Hey, I'm good and you?" she asks.

"I'm good. I'm even better now that I see you," he says giving me a firm hug.

"Look, whenever you get home call me or come over cause I wanna spend some time with you."

"I can't cause I gotta work tonight which is a bummer seeing that I don't get off until 9," I say giving him the Babyface.

"Well, seeing the library is a public place how about he chills with you at work?" Julia asks finally butting in.

"Sounds like a plan to me. Meet me at the house and we can take my car down then we can go out to dinner after work," he says walking away backward, "And don't worry dinners on me.

I shake my head 'ok' while mugging Julia.

"What I was just trying to help out. If I had not of not, you would've lost him," she pleads as she follows behind me.

"Look, we gotta get to class," I say as I try to sound mad with a little smirk on my face.

On the way there she pleads, begs and whines, which doesn't stop the silent treatment I'm giving her.

"Look Demonte, I'm your girl and as your girl, I just wanna see you happy. Is that a crime?"

"No, but what is a crime is how you tried to put the situation on front street," I tell her with a smile.

"Is there something you would like to share with the class, Mr. Bryant?" Mr. Lee asks.

"Ugh no, sir. I apologize."

I hear Julia laugh, but I didn't because I'm tired of being picked on, plus, I had an at work date with my main man. The rest of the class went by really quick because my mind keeps wondering back to the conversation we had on the lawn. When the class is finally over I said bye to Julia and meet Carlos at the house like planned.

"Are you ready?" he asks when I pull up.

"Ugh, yeah, I just gotta go grab my phone. Is that ok?" I ask playfully.

"Yeah go right ahead."

We laugh as we walk up the walkway. Thank God everybody is still at work because I don't feel like getting drilled. Once in the house, I run to my room to grab my phone off my desk where I left it to check my notifications and to my surprise it's empty.

"Hey, Carlos, didn't you say you called me earlier?" I ask from my room while he was roaming around up front.

"With a text message, why?"

I check my messages and there it is, a message from Carlos that I never read or open with a text message from my mom reminding us about the carpet cleaners and my aunt house sitting. Right then and there I know for a fact that my aunt went through my phone. I walk into the living room where he is with an attitude.

"What's wrong?" he asks.

"I think my aunt went through my phone which would explain that pick and hang up from earlier."

"Look, let me get you to work and we'll figure this out later, ok?"

"OK, I guess," I say as I follow him to the front door.

On the way there we didn't say anything but I knew he wanted to say something because he just keeps looking over at me. But when we finally pull in I just sit there because I wanna call off and spend the rest of my day with Carlos.

"Well, we're here. Are you sure you wanna go to work?" he asks me with a smile.

"Yeah, why not, cause I need the money homie. I got a quick shift today," I tell him with a smile.

We start walking towards the building and I can see Craig shelving books from the window and for some reason he knew I was down here. Carlos all of a sudden grabs my hand and I look at him and I can tell he notices because his facial expression completely changed. I burst out laughing and he looks at me.

"What's so funny?" he asks.

"Nothing," I say holding back my laugh.

Okay, I'm not go lie, he IS so adorable looking when he got a little mad but I just don't wanna tell him that.

I look over at him when we get on the elevator and I can tell he's mad about something because when he gets mad the vein in his forehead pops out.

"What's wrong?" I ask.

"You work with him?" he asks.

"Who, Craig? Yea why?"

"Demonte, that's my crazy ex. I have been meaning to tell you but I figured he didn't work here anymore so I didn't say anything babe. I swear I wasn't trying to hide it from you," he tells me looking dead in the eyes.

The elevator finally gets to the floor of my department so we step off but before we turn the corner I pull him to the side.

"Look, I trust but is there anything you're not telling me?" I ask him.

"There's nothing else but the fact he tried to kill me. Look I'll just come back when you get off cause I don't feel too comfortable here."

"Ok, I'll just call you when I get off okay?"

"OK sounds like a plan, but Demonte, I'm really sorry," he tells me with a really sad face.

"Don't be I completely understand. I don't wanna put you in an uncomfortable situation. So get going cause my shifts about to start."

He leans in to give me a hug and kiss then heads to the elevator. I turn around to head to the clock and find Craig by a shelf staring my direction with a mean mug face which made me walk even faster.

"Hey, Demonte. How are you?" Gina asks when I get to the back.

"Hey, Gina. I'm good and you?" I ask.

"Not too bad just living the dream. I got some books for you and Craig to shelve but from the looks of it, he did majority of them. Just finish these and we'll go from there," she tells me.

"Alrighty then. Let the games begin."

After she walks away, I hear somebody walk into the back and just to my luck its Craig. When I notice it's him I try to hurry and push the cart to the front but we crossed paths anyway.

"Hey Demonte, how are you?" he asks.

"Hey, Craig, I'm good and you?"

"I'm good just pulling in some overtime," he says, "but I got a question and please promise you won't get mad."

"It depends on what it is?" I tell him. I just know it's about Carlos and I really don't wanna start something nor do I wanna get in the middle of anything.

"Who is Carlos to you?" he asks.

My blood begins to boil and I can feel my attitude flair.

"Look, let's get one thing straight right here right now. I'm not going there with you about me and Carlos' relationship so do not even begin to ask questions. You got it?"

"I'm so sorry. I didn't mean to offend you," He starts to say. Before he can finish I just walked away.

During my entire shift, I was quiet and thankfully if it wasn't worked related nobody said anything to me. I do wonder if he said anything to anybody about it because it took him a long time to clock out and leave. I can't believe he would try to question me about Carlos. I texted him to let him my shift was almost over and Craig is gone.

"Demonte, after you are done, you can leave," Gina says from her office.

"Ok," I respond.

I feel my phone vibrate letting me know I had a text message. It was a message from Carlos saying, "Babe where are you…?" I respond saying, "Babe I'm clocking out…. B out n a sec…. ;-)."

"Okay everybody, I'm done and I'm out. See y'all next week," I say running towards the door not even waiting for a response.

Chapter Eight

Wait, What?!?!?!?!?

As soon as I get out to the waiting area, I see Carlos but he is not alone. I can tell it's intense because the veins are popping out of Carlos' forehead which is not a good sign. As I get closer I see that the person that was making him mad was Craig which started to piss me off. When I finally get close enough I walk up on Carlos to give him a kiss on the cheek while mean mugging Craig.

"Is everything okay Baby?" I ask Carlos, looking Craig dead in the eyes. I swear if looks could kill, Craig would be so dead.

"Yeah, Babe. I was just telling Craig that I'm in a relationship with you and that he needs to knock the thought of us getting back together out of his head. Right, Craig?" he explains.

All Craig can do is just stand there, stuck for words, and feel stupid.

"Right, Craig?" I ask, knowing it is pissing him off even more. Without a saying a word Craig storms off.

"Yeah, of course. I can respect that and I'm so sorry that this had to be done," he says turning away.

Without looking at Carlos, I begin to walk towards the car without saying a word and I can tell that he is trying to keep up.

"Babe, wait up," he says out of breath. He finally catches up to me and grabs my arm.

"What? I thought we had a date to get to?" I say without noticing my tone. I can tell that he is hurt by it.

"Baby, nothing happened. I swear, NOTHING HAPPENED!" he pleads.

"Did I say anything happened?"

"You don't have to. Your attitude says it all."

"I don't have an attitude. I'm just a little tired and ready to go out to eat."

We finally reach the car. I notice something big and red in the passenger seat.

"Baby, what's this in the car?" I ask.

"Oh, I don't know. Check it out," he responds.

I open the door and there it is: a beautiful bouquet of roses with my name on the card, big as day. I feel my face turning red, hot, and wet then I feel him wrapping his arms around me. I turn towards him and all I see is his teeth.

"Baby, I feel so stupid for going off like that."

He walks over to me covering my lips, "It's okay, Baby."

"Then what really happened back there?"

He turns back towards me but looks like he wants to cry.

"Baby, if I tell you, will you promise you won't get mad?"

I stand there contemplating his face, his actions and the fact of me willing to believe him.

"Baby, do you?" he asks imploring.

"You got fifteen seconds, GO!"

"Ok, so I was sitting in the lobby, waiting on you. He approaches me asking me about my mother and stuff. That's when he started trying to get back with me and saying he is so sorry about how much he misses me. I quickly brushed him off but he came back harder, but that's when you came out."

I can tell that is telling the truth because he looks me dead in the eyes with those puppy dog eyes. I just roll my eyes getting in the car. The whole ride to our date I didn't say a mumbling word to him but he is constantly trying to get me to talk. I don't know why the situation bothers me so much because I feel as if I know he wouldn't cheat but then there is another side of me that believes otherwise. I love him, I really, do but there is a lot of emotional damage that I will need to recover from before I can trust another man again.

We finally pull up to the parking lot of the park, which confused me because I just knew we were going to a restaurant.

"So, uh, where are we going?" I ask.

"You are just gonna have to wait and see, Mr. Impatient."

Now everybody and they mama know I'm impatient, so why tease me? I try to wait patiently but it's to the point where I'm getting agitated, so I sigh hard.

"I'll ask you again; where are going in the park?"

He doesn't respond but parks in the nearest parking spot, gets out to open my door like the perfect gentleman and motions for me to get out of the car. But like a stubborn mule, I refuse to get out.

"Where are we going because I'm not getting out until you tell me?!?"

He leans into the car and pulls me out, carrying me towards the woods. Now I'm really getting scared because I don't know what's going on so I just close my eyes, praying that everything turns out ok.

"Baby, look what I did for us," he says putting me down.

I turn to see a perfect little picnic laid out on a blanket with a bouquet of roses with rose petals spelling 'I LOVE YOU, BABY'. Now he got me over here feeling stupid as hell because he wants to be all romantic but I'm not going fold yet.

"Aww, how cute Baby. I love it, Baby, but when did you have time to do all of this considering you had a super busy day? Unless you were lying to me the whole time and was running around Cincinnati looking for all of these?"

"Baby, just say 'thank you' and eat. You just know the perfect way to ruin the mood. All I wanted to do is eat, talk, cuddle, and star gaze. But, no, you wanna question every little move I make. Can you just show some appreciation?" he asks, looking at me with an attitude.

"Ok, ok, ok you are right. I apologize. So what's in the basket?" I ask while we get down on the blanket.

"Well, I got us some sandwiches, chips n dip, your favorite Dr. Pepper, and for dessert, I got us chess pie. I know it's nothing fancy, but it's a little something."

"It's perfect and yes I do appreciate it, Carlos."

He smiles and turns away because he starts to blush a little. Everything is telling me he's the one, but I just don't why I can't trust him emotionally. It's going to be a rough ride but I'm ready to ride.

"So, what do you have planned for your life after graduation?" Carlos ask.

"Oh, I don't know anymore because I wanted to take over my grandfather's stores in Alabama but I think I wanna become an author and touch somebody with my writing. I wanna use my past and talent to guide someone, somewhere, to a brighter future."

I start to feel insecure and stop talking, which I think he can tell because he embraces me in his arms.

"Why do you make it so easy to tell you anything?"

"Well, why do make it so easy to want to know more about you?"

"I wouldn't even know how to answer because I've been hurt so much. I mean I want you in my life and my world but I'm scared."

"Baby, I love you. I promise you I do. Why can't you see that? I will do almost anything for you cause you are my world, my life."

I can see in his eyes that he is telling the truth but I really don't know how to respond. I don't know where to begin to express my happiness of being with him without expressing my pain. I just stare off into space hoping not to cry but that's when he gets up and pulls me up with him.

"Where are we going?" I ask.

"Just come with me; I wanna show you something."

We start walking towards the open fields of trees and he reaches for his pocket knife which really makes me wanna run for my life but I know I'm safe with him.

"What are you about to do?"

"You'll see," he says with a smirk.

He starts carving what looks like a rectangle into the bark of the tree. Then he goes to carve letters into it, so I step closer to get a better view and what I see is the cutest thing. He carved a heart and our names through it on the tree and like always I tear up like a Baby. I walk over to say hi, to embrace in a hug and gives me a kiss on the forehead.

"Ready to go?" he asks. I shake my head 'yes' while resting my head in his chest.

We get back the car where he opened the door for me again. At this point, I really don't know how to feel so when he finally gets in and starts the car I just simply grab his hand. The ride back to my house is longer than usual and silent because neither one of us knew what to say without ticking me off. I don't wanna scare him away with my anger issue but where do I go from here.

"What's really wrong, Baby?" he asks looking me dead in the eyes.

Now I know I'm wearing my emotions on my face. I know he will understand that I'm afraid to tell my mom that I'm in love with a person of the same sex. I'm afraid that it would break my mother's heart and my brother would disown me. What do I do? What should I say? How would they even find out?

"Baby, if I ask you a question would you be honest?" I ask.

"I have been so far, so why stop now?" he asks.

Just the way he answered lets me know that he is mad about something. I wish he would understand how hard this is on me but it's hard to explain this someone that is openly gay with his family. I could really use his help with coming out of the closet but instead of arguing.

"Baby, I need your help with something. Do you remember how I told my brother that I was gay?" I ask him.

"Yeah, why?" he asks sarcastically.

"Well, can you please be there with me when I tell my mother?"

He continues to drive looking straight out of the windshield.

"Baby, did you hear me?" I ask.

"What took you so long to ask?"

"I didn't know how you would react. I mean you are openly gay with your mother which makes it easy for you to be yourself. I, on the other hand; I just can't do it alone especially not now. Not when everything is starting to look up and promising for me."

"Well, how could everything be looking up for you when you are carrying such a heavy burden?"

It's moments like this that really want to make me wanna punch him dead in his mouth. Why does everything gotta have a smart question behind it? I'll never know with him. I stall for a minute to think of an answer but nothing came to me because he's right. How could really start looking up for me when I'm hiding a burden like this?

"Baby, just promise me that when the time comes, you'll be there."

"You got it," he says with a huge smile on his face.

We finally get to my house, where he politely pulls up in front of my house, and I'm getting really nervous. And to my surprise, he gets out of the car to open my door, holding out his hands out for mine. I'm really stuck because I actually have a good man and I'm afraid to accept him because of my own insecurities. I grabbed his hand and got out of the car.

"So, did you enjoy yourself tonight?" he asks.

"Well," I paused.

"Yes, no, maybe?"

Aww, now he is super nervous. Leaving a guy wondering if you truly enjoyed yourself will have any guy on edge. Oh, how will I enjoy this. I am going to tease the living hell out of him but then he hits me with the puppy dog face when we get to my door.

"Well, ok. Yes, Carlos, I enjoyed myself."

"Thank goodness, because I was a little worried. I'm not used to planning romantic picnics or dates. Demonte, I really care about you and it makes me so happy that you asked me to be there with you when you come out," he tells me.

By this time, I'm being held in his arms, which makes the moment even more romantic.

"I really don't know what to say but thank you. I really gotta go though cause I have a busy day tomorrow."

"Call me tomorrow then?" he asks giving me a kiss on the forehead.

"Okay, I will," I say trying to finding my keys.

He starts to walk towards his house but then turns to watch me walk in the house with a smile on his face. I swear he's the one I've been waiting for and I finally got him. I finally get into the house and the house is quite which means they are sleep. I take a shower and lay my bad praying that he texts me first.

"Good night…Baby," Carlos texts me.

"Night."

Morning finally comes and I beat the crack of dawn for a jog. I choose the same park that me and Carlos had our first date for some strange reason. I start my motivational playlist and stretches and then off I go. Feelings from the night before started to take over my body and paralyze me again. I even noticed the same tree that Carlos carved our names in and there it comes, a stream of tears. Just then I start to feel uncomfortable and hearing leaves crumble up behind me as if somebody is walking up behind me. Just then, two hands grab me from behind which made me turn around thinking it was Carlos but to my surprise, it was Ryan.

"WAT THE HELL?!" I shout out to him

"Demonte, please just listen for a minute," Ryan says to me.

"Look, we have absolutely nothing to talk about. How and when did you get here? Why are you here?"

After all of this time, I actually thought I was developing some kind of withdraw from him be imagining him but he is actually here. My first instinct is to call Carlos and the police but I'm so nervous and scared, fear takes over my body while shutting down the functional part of my brain. All I keep asking is, "Why are you here?"

"I just had to reclaim you as my boyfriend, my life," he replies grabbing my arm.

"You really are crazy. Just leave me alone before I get another restraining order. I'm pretty sure I made myself clear before leaving Birmingham that I didn't want anything to do with you," I tell him snatching arm out of his hand.

When I finally regain control of my body, I ran off without giving that maniac a chance to say anything else. I grab my phone to call Craig but Briana call intervened.

"Hey Demonte," I hear her say with so much joy.

"Hey Briana," I say.

"What's wrong?" she asks.

"Um, well, you won't believe it even you were here to see it."

"Okay, now you are scaring me, Demonte. What happened?"

"Well, while I was on my jog, I ran into Ryan."

It felt as if time had stopped once I repeated out loud. It seems as if I could never get away from my past. I try so hard to change my present but my pass won't leave me alone long enough to enjoy it.

"Briana, are you still there?" I finally ask.

"I'm just speechless. I can't believe he followed you all the way back to Cincinnati. Are you okay?"

"Yeah. I left without giving him a chance to speak. But look, I'll call you after I finish this jog."

"Okay, bye."

The more I think about what was said and the conversation itself, I can't help but run harder, faster. Before I knew it, I was home. To my surprise, my mother is at home at the table drinking tea as if she was waiting for me.

"Hey Ma," I say.

"Hello Demonte," she says in a monotone voice.

When she spoke to me, it sends chills through my body.

"You okay?" I ask her.

"Yeah, everything's okay. Just the fact that I got word about someone I really care about. So tell me Demonte, are you by any chance gay?"

I felt my head spinning and my throat getting dry. I can't believe my mother just asked me that. I turn to her to answer but that's when my brother walks into the room. We both shot each other looks that let us know what's going on.

"Um, uh, well," I say and from the looks of it my brother senses my pain and sits down.

"Ma, before you get mad, me and Demonte know the answer to that question," Trey says.

Oh yeah, throw me under the bus while you at it while you at. I simply lose my train of thought. What should I do? What should I say? Everything in me is screaming tell her but I can't hold it in no more. It is draining everything out of me because I don't know how to tell the woman that gave birth to me and has loved me all of my life that I'm gay. I started to fill numb and decided to sit down with them.

"Well, Ma, I kinda am gay," I tell her.

The look on her face lets me know that she is not impressed with the answer I gave her. After sitting there for three minutes, got up and left to go to her room slamming her bedroom door. My brother and I sit there looking at each other in complete astonishment and confused. I went to my room and crawled into my bed to cry eyes but that's when I felt Trey wrap his arms around me.

"Why me, Trey?" I ask him.

"Bra, I told you I got your back," he tells me.

"I just can't believe that she just left like that. I mean she just didn't say a mumbling word."

I started to cry even harder because I officially hurt my mother with something I can't recover from. I cried myself to sleep once again.

Chapter Nine

I Spy A Snitch

I woke up the next morning in bed alone except for the huge bags under my eyes. I'm so glad my brother is here to comfort me because I wouldn't have made it through the night. I finally got the strength to barely crawl out of bed. I grabbed my phone to check my emails, texts and missed calls.

"When you wake up, check and see if I'm still home… We need to finish talking about you," a text says from Trey.

I wish this situation would just go away without any memory of it happening. I go to my mom's room first and I can tell she didn't sleep in her room if she even stayed home at all. I go to Trey's room to see if he's there but he's not and I don't hear a T.V. playing in the house so that means I'm home alone.

The pain I feel is unbearable because I feel like I'm hurting the two people I care about. I check the kitchen for breakfast and to my surprise, nothing. I check my watch and see that I have to stop and pick up breakfast before work.

"Good Morning! I love you…Tae," I text Trey.

I think I'm suffering from some type of depression because I'm always more depressed than happy which is hurtful. I just hope things get better as we get through this. When I start to just lay there in my bed, I get a text from Carlos asking me do I want to go to the mall.

"How about a quick breakfast because I gotta go to work," I reply.

"Sure."

I get a little energy and excited because I actually want to see him but didn't know how to ask him over after what happened. When my home screen comes up showing the picture Carlos and me, I started to cry and smile at the same time. Words can't explain how happy I am to be with a man as beautiful as him but I wonder if the feelings are mutual. I poke through my closet looking for the perfect hook up to impress him with. After forty-five minutes and twenty minutes, I finally decide on an all blue hook up with a pair of all blue Nike's with all white soles to match. He finally texts me and asks if I was ready. I reply "yes", grab my jacket and ran out the door. As I walk out the door, I notice a bouquet of white roses.

"For you, Baby," he says handing me the flowers and a kiss.

OH MY GOSH! This boy smells so good that I get tongue-tied.

"Thanks, Baby. How's your morning?" I ask.

"Mines great but you look like hell. What's wrong?"

"Baby, it happened. My aunt told my mom that I'm gay," I tell him tearing up.

He grabs me immediately and lets me cry on his shoulder like the man he is. It's moments like this that makes me appreciate him even more.

"Baby, stop crying because you are with me now ok," he says directing me into the car.

When he gets in the car, he starts the engine and reaches his hand out for mines and like a punk, I accept quickly.

"Are you okay now, Baby?" he asks quietly.

"I'm hurt because this is not how I wanted to tell her. Why me?"

"I don't know. Out of spite, maybe?"

I shrug my shoulders. I wish I didn't have to work today because I know I'll have an attitude tonight. I now know for a fact he is trying to cheer me up because we are pulling up into my favorite breakfast restaurant. He finds the perfect parking spot by the front door which is great by me. As usual, he gets out first to open the car door like the perfect gentlemen and walk me to the door which makes me feel super special in every way. I wish moments like this would last forever and all my troubles would fade away.

"Thank you so much, Baby. This breakfast uplifted my spirit and I really did need this. But enough about me, how's school?" I ask him.

"You know I will always be there for you. As far as school, everything is great. My grades are good and my tuition is covered. I've really been thinking about the break in between semesters and I was hoping that we could go on a little vacation. What do you think?" he states.

"That sounds wonderful. But to where, Babe?" I ask looking surprised.

"I really haven't put that much thought into the where yet. I just know that I need a vacation and I want to spend it with you."

"There you go trying to be all romantic and stuff. How about Atlanta or maybe Miami?" I inquire.

"Anywhere with you is perfect with me. Demonte, I mean, you make me feel alive again. You make me feel as if anything is possible with you by my side. Answer this for me, do you really love me like you say you do?" he asks looking me dead in the eyes as if he was trying to mesmerize me.

"Baby, you are all I think about night and day. With you, I can finally be myself and nobody else but me."

We both sit there holding each other's hand with tears rolling down our cheeks. I can't believe that we are having a moment like this. All I know is that I'm glad that it's happening now after what happened last night. This is all I need to hear to make it through the day at work. Our food finally comes and we both are that hungry that we scarf our food down.

I promise you when I look at him, I see an angel, my shield. Am I putting too much into this relationship or am I holding too much from him? He looks up at me with a little syrup on his chin. I chuckle while he looks at me confused so I whip the syrup off.

"Thanks, Babe," he says with a smile.

"So, what are your plans for today?" I ask.

"Um, nothing really. Just studying and working out. I'll wait for you if you want me too."

"Sure. I get off at 6 and I'll probably be getting home at 6:30. Is that cool?"

"I'll just come get you since we took my car?" he offers.

"How about no because I don't want you near or around Craig. I'll meet you at the house like I said."

"Demonte Bryant, I'll meet you at work like I said. I don't have to come into the building, I'll call you when I pull up. End of discussion."

"Oh, I love it when you take charge," I say with sarcasm.

He shoots me a look as if wants to punch me. I can't believe he is mad that I said that, but he knows how I am. I just look out the window just praying that the comment I just made doesn't cause us to argue on our way to my job. He asks the waitress for the check while we finish up our food so I reach into my bag to get my wallet.

"What are you doing?" he asks.

"Getting my wallet, why?"

"No, Baby I'm paying. Put your money up and stop tripping."

I grab his hand and start caressing it hoping that this calms him because I know he wants to say something smart. He pays for the food and we head to the car where as usual he opens the door.

"So, why don't you want me to come to get you?" he asks.

"Because I don't need or want the extra drama at work. Plus, after what you told me he did to you, I don't wanna have to jack him up and lose my freedom," I say to him giving him the biggest smile ever.

He gives me a smirk that tells me that he feels where I'm coming from. We are quietly cruising downtown, holding hands and listening to Tank better known as my favorite male artist. After like ten minutes of driving, we finally pull up to the library.

"Have a good day at work and try not to make anybody come up missing," he says laughing leaning over to give me a kiss.

"I'll try Baby, but I'm not making any type of promises," I tell him getting out of the car.

When I get out, I look up at the department like I always do when I get out of the car and notice Craig watching me. I really don't know how much he saw, but I know it is making me feel uncomfortable. When he notices that I see him, he walks away mean mugging.

"And it begins," I mumble to myself.

Chapter Ten

Break Out!

Everything seems to be okay here in the department but I'm still keeping my eye on Craig. I'm not trying to rub anybody the wrong but if he approaches Carlos, I promise I will lose it on him. I push my cart and start my route as usual but I stop by the department front desk to talk to Gina and Alice.

"Hey, Ladies, how are y'all doing today?" I ask.

"I'm great," they say in unison.

"So, I have a question about the holiday party. Can we bring a guest with us?" I ask.

"Yeah, but you can only bring one guest though because of the budget for the party," Gina says.

"I'm so excited about it that I can't wait," I say.

"Me too. So, Demonte, are you bringing that lucky person that claims your heart?" Alice asks.

Wait, WHAT?!?!?!?! Keep calm Demonte and breath. Did she just ask about Carlos? My Carlos, at that?

"Maybe. That's if he doesn't have to work that night," I stutter responding.

"Can't wait to meet him," she says.

"Well ladies, I hate to cut this short but I gotta get these shelved."

"Alright Demonte," Gina responds.

For some reason, I start feeling uncomfortable around Alice. I don't know why but I guess it's because of the way she was asking about Carlos. But with the feelings I have, it doesn't stop me from wearing the biggest smile on my face. That's my problem, I can't get or stay mad at Carlos because he made his mark in my heart as my lover, my best friend, my world. While I'm shelving in my own little world, I see Craig walk out from the back, texting somebody. He looks up towards me and makes his way towards me. I try to avoid him by moving to another part of the department but he follows me.

"Hey, Demonte. Can we talk please?" he says.

I pretend as if I didn't hear him but he continues to talk.

"Demonte, I'm so sorry for overstepping my boundaries with Carlos. It's just that I'm still in love with him and it kinda threw me off to see that he has moved on without me," he says.

By this time, I'm starting to lose my cool with him and this situation so I roll my eyes and turn towards him.

"Look, I'm done with and this whole situation. If I was you, I would be too. I ain't got nothing else to say to you but stay your ass away from me and my boyfriend. Do I make myself clear?"

He nods his head letting me know he gets it. After I see that, I walk off pushing my empty cart to the back. If it's not one thing, it's another. I wish Carlos never existed or at least not work here. While I glance over at the front desk, I peep that Alice and Gina are trying to secretly find out what's going on but Craig continues to leave the department without uttering a word.

"Hey, Demonte, wait up!" I hear Alice say as she runs behind me.

"Yes, Alice," I say feeling extra aggravated.

"Everything ok?" she asks.

I just stand there, quiet, trying to fight back the tears of frustration but it's no use because I feel the tears that feel like fire.

"Um, yeah kind of but I need time to wrap my mind around some things," I tell her hoping that would send her off.

"Something is not right between Carlos and you. What's going on?"

"Well, um it has something to do with my boyfriend."

"What does Carlos have to do with you and your boyfriend?"

"Carlos' ex-boyfriend is my current boyfriend and ever since I found out, things haven't been right since between us."

By now my face is covered in tears. Alice embraces me with the tightest hug as if she could feel my pain. I can't believe that I just told a complete stranger about my relationship which makes me feel very vulnerable. I look around to make sure we were alone which it looks like we are.

"I just don't want anything to happen that could possibly affect me here at work or personally with Carlos," I briefly tell her.

"I completely understand. Stay with Carlos because he is your man and nothing should come between the two of you especially if you two genuinely love each other. Look, I gotta get back on the floor and help Gina. If you ever need to talk, I'm here for you," she tells me before walking to the door.

I see that the clock says that I have ten minutes left of my shift, so I rush to finish everything. When I finally do, I gather my things and head to the front desk like I always do before leaving.

"Ok Ladies, I'm out of here. Do you need anything else before I leave?" I ask.

"No, everything looks great from here. See you at the Christmas party?" Gina ask.

"Um, yeah sure. I don't see why not."

Just then my phone vibrates letting me know that I have an incoming phone call and luckily, it's from Carlos.

"I will see you guys later at the party. This is my ride calling," I say walking backwards towards the staircase.

"Bye Demonte," I hear them say.

I wave bye, answering the phone.

"Hey, Baby. You outside?" I answer.

"Yeah, Baby. I'm on the Vine Street exit."

"Okay, I'll be right out," I warn him hanging up the phone.

I look down for two seconds to put my phone in my bag and that's when I run into Craig.

"Look, Demonte, whatever you do with Carlos in your spare time is none of my business but DO NOT TRY AND FLAUNT IT IN MY FACE. I already had what he is offering you; the candlelit picnic dinners, the romantic dinner movie dates, I had it already. Technically, I still get it because he is not completely over me and that's why he tried to cover that little conversation we had up because he didn't want you to find out. I like how you are trying to play 'Super Boyfriend,' but Sweetie stop while you are ahead because I win and you lose," he says walking away leaving me standing there with my mouth wide open.

I could not do anything nor say anything. I cannot believe what I just heard and it's making me feel like a ton of bricks just fell out of the sky and crushed me in the process. I see Carlos calling me again, so I rush down the steps to the car. When I finally get down there, I see him standing outside the passenger side of the car as always.

"Hey Baby," he says leaning in for a kiss.

Before I knew it, I had smack him. I literally smack the left side of his face with tears rolling down my face.

"WHAT THE HELL, DEMONTE!"

"How in the hell do you sit here and try to play me with your ex is what the hell," I shout.

At this moment I feel so betrayed by the one guy I called my lover.

"What are you talking about?"

"Carlos, please stop faking it. He told me everything about the picnics and the romantic dinners that you failed to tell me about. How could you?" I asked walking towards the cab stand in front of the library.

"Demonte, wait up!"

I just keep walking because I don't want to hear any more lies that he felt like I needed to hear, because I am not about to go through this with him.

"Demonte!" I hear him screaming after me but I continue to get into the cab staring him dead in the face.

"1920 Random Road," I tell the cab driver.

As I look back out of the back windshield, I see him standing in the middle of the road with tears in his eyes. I can't believe that this happens to me again. I put all of my trust into somebody that I 'trusted'. It's okay though because I'm done with him. I finally get home to see that I beat him home, but my brother is at the house. I can't deal with looking at him with this going on. I pay the driver and ran into the house where my brother was waiting for me in the living room.

"Sup, Trey?" I say walking in the house.

"Question is what is up with you and Carlos?" he asks.

Okay, the lame called my brother like a lame. I thought we were past that stage in life where we ran to the family behind each other's back.

"What are you talking about?" me asking acting clueless.

"Nothing. I just thought he was supposed to pick you up from work. At least that's what he told me when I saw him earlier."

Okay, good shot. This means he didn't call and Trey thinks we are still lovie dovie.

"Something came up on his end, so I caught a cab," I tell him.

"Well, why didn't you call me?"

"Cause I know you are tired and I didn't want to disturb you on your off day. I gotta though 'cause I got to catch up on my exam prep," I tell him while I run off to my room.

I threw my bag on my bed, close the door and just lost. Tears are just rolling down my eyes one after another. Why me? Why now? I walk over to my window to see if he's home and to my surprise, I see him in his jogging suit with somebody else. I can tell that he is 'hurt' but who cares?

Chapter Eleven

Heartbreak Hotel

My alarm is screaming at the same time it does every morning, but today I just ignore it. My heart is still throbbing from yesterday and my head feels like a bullet is sitting in my forehead. I just lay motionless in my bed because I just can't get myself to get dress or go to school and work because I feel betrayed by the one I thought I could trust with my feelings. I hear a knock on my door, but I ignore that too but then I hear my door open.

"Hey, you ain't going to school?" I hear my brother ask.

"Does it even matter? Mama ain't talking cause she's mad at me and Carlos ain't talking to me cause I'm mad at him. What a life?"

"What happened in paradise now?" he asks in a joking way.

"I caught, well more like was told, that he's been cheating on me with his ex. Matter of fact they were still talking when we met or so he says."

The more I tell him, the more it hurts. I still can't believe that Craig was bold enough to tell me what was going on. Our first big argument since we've been together but it looks like I'm the only suffering. Just then, my phone starts to vibrate letting me know that I have a phone call and to my surprise it's Carlos. I ignore of course.

"Ain't you go answer that?" my brother asks.

"No, I'll make him suffer a little. Got any plans for today?"

"Ugh, no just lay around the house like a lazy bum. Why?"

"Lunch on me today. Where you wanna go?"

"To the pizzeria would be cool. Why are you being so nice all of a sudden?"

"What? I can't treat my only brother to lunch?"

"Why not? I'm about to go get dressed."

"Aight, but be ready in like an hour."

"Aight."

When my brother finally leaves my room, my phone vibrates again, telling me it's him calling again with three text messages. But once again, I ignore and continue to get ready. I get the shower at the temp that I like it and get ready to hop in but then I get another phone call and it's not Carlos; it's Ryan. My heart drops and my head starts to spin out of control making it hard to keep my balance. He calls two more and sends me countless text messages in a matter of seconds. I just hop in the shower and ignore them both.

"Hey, you ready?" my brother calls from the living room.

"Yeah, Man just calm down," I say grabbing my designer book bag.

"What took you so long?" he asks when I get near the living room.

"You just can't rush perfection, so remember that for future references," I say laughing.

"Haha, funny. Man, let's go before the lunch rush hits."

"Aight, let's go before I uppercut you into the restaurant," I say as I locked the door behind us.

I look over and I see Carlos walking out of his house with the same guy I saw him with the other day. As I stand here, staring at him in confusion and hurt, I wonder if he knows how much he is hurting me right now? Before he could make his way to me or say a word to me, I ran to my car.

"Are you aight? I mean I know you just say yo boy but why are you running from him?" he asks when I get in the car.

"I mean I'm ok; it just hurts like hell. How could this happen to me again?"

Just then, my phone vibrates again letting me know that I was receiving a phone call and to my surprise, it is Carlos calling from his car. I ignore the call of course but I wanted to answer so badly but it would be too painful to talk to him.

"Look, Demonte, he loves you and you love him. So why fight it?"

I sit on the driver side quietly and decide to start the car to pull off. It's nothing I could say because my brother is right; I do love him and I know that he loves me but why lie to me. We drive to the pizzeria in silence for the longest because I don't know what to say. We finally get to the pizzeria and grab our usual sit by the big screen to catch the game but continue to say nothing to each other.

"Look, I know you are hurting right now but tell him the truth and see what really is going. I really don't think that he would ever hurt intentionally because he cares too much about you," he says.

"Trey, can we just enjoy the night and forget all about him because I still haven't fully forgiven him yet."

"I understand and I'll leave it alone. So, how's work and school going?" he asks.

"Everything's great. I'm passing all of my classes and everyone at work is nice," I tell him as we get ready to order.

"That's good. So, what are your plans after graduation?"

"I don't know anymore, I really don't. I'm at the point where I'm taking it step by step because I'm not trying to lose my way in life trying to please everybody," I tell him.

"I know 'cause I feel like I lost my way trying to please Mama and Daddy. But the one thing I don't regret is protecting you. I know that you just my little but brother but sometimes you scare me and I just wanna make sure you okay."

Just then the food finally arrives ruining the emotional brother moment but I can tell that he is sincere about what he is saying. In a way I see where he's coming from but why are you telling me this now? Something is wrong and he is trying to avoid telling me which is not cool because I tell him everything. Trust me, I'll find out. As we sit here eating, I can see a lot of me in my brother which helps me better understand why he doesn't tell me everything that is going on with him but I wish he would let me help him. I guess he got it figured all cause he sure ain't telling me. We finally leave the restaurant the same exact way we came, silent.

We finally get to the house and I go first to unlock the door but I stop. I look over at his house, hoping to see him one last time before the day is over but I guess I'm not. I can see me run across the yard the day I helped them with the groceries and he greeted me with a kiss or the day he greeted me at the end of my walk-way with a bouquet of flowers. I could feel tears roll down my right cheek.

"You okay?" my brother asks in a concerned voice which snaps me out of my daydream.

"Uh, yeah. I'm just looking for the right key."

I finally unlock the door and beeline it to my room. We didn't say anything because it felt as if our souls are doing all of the talking which is normal for us.

"So, do wanna talk about what's bothering you?" I ask when I get to his bedroom door.

"Nope, nothing that I can think of. Why?" he says.

"Trey, stop playing dumb. I know you got something that you wanna tell me because of that whole little speech you gave me at the pizzeria. You know that's a dead giveaway that something is bothering you. Now, what's going on?"

He sits at the edge of his bed quietly, looking at the wall. By the way his facial expression just changed, I know it's something serious.

"She's pregnant," he says holding back tears.

"Who's pregnant?" I ask confused.

"Jackie is pregnant and she is telling me that it's mine."

"Well, is it yours? I always told you to wrap it up but, nooo, nobody wanna listen to the gay dude like he ain't take sex ed in school."

See, Jackie is his new girlfriend who irks my nerve and she knows she does. She kinda looks like a jacked up version of Jennifer Hudson; from the waist up, she looks like the old JHud but waist down, she looks like the new JHud and I don't mean that in a sexy way.

"Demonte, this is not even funny."

"Does it look like I'm laughing? You act like she trying to have an abortion or give it up for adoption," I say walking towards him.

Before I know it, he looks at me covered in tears shacking.

"Trey, what's wrong?" I ask getting nervously.

"She's talking about getting an abortion."

As soon as he said it, it feels as if a ton of bricks fell on top of me. I sit there not knowing what to say because I don't even know how I'm feeling this split second. Before I knew it, I begin to cry and grabbing him.

"If I got anything to do with it, she's not and that's a promise," I tell him.

We cry for another half hour and I finally to my room to spy on Craig's house with the binoculars I just bought. Yeah, call me crazy but I gotta make sure ok from a distance. When I finally get to my room I hear a car pull up in his driveway which made me run to my window faster. I get there, binoculars in hand; to see if he was alone and to my surprise, he was still with the dude from earlier. So I zoom in to get a clear view of the persons face and to my surprise it was Ryan. I drop the binoculars while Trey is walking by my door which makes him walk in.

"What's wrong?" he asks.

"Either I'm high on some type drug or Ryan just got out of the car with Craig," I tell him.

He grabs the binoculars and looks into that direction.

"Yeah, that's him."

I can't believe that this is happening right now. Not only did my ex follow me into my new life away from him but he has weaseled his way into my relationship.

"Not here, not now. I can't have him screwing this part of my life up to. I can't believe he is doing this to me," I say typing up a text to send to Carlos.

"What are you doing?" he asks.

"Oh nothing, just telling Carlos how I really feel."

"Don't say something now that you may regret later. I'm trying to help save your relationship here," he warns me.

When he says that, I just simply through my phone on my bed.

"I'm going to the park. I'll be back before dinner."

The drive here seems as if I drove at light year speed because I don't remember the drive. I walk the flower petals and sniff the flowers that were still part of a bush. The view is beautiful as always. It takes the pain that I'm feeling away and replace it with happiness. I continue walking down the familiar path until I ran into the very tree that reflected my pain. The same tree that Carlos carved our names into which is so painful to look at. Rag and anger ran through my system which drives to pick up a rock to deface it until my hands begin to bleed. When I notice the blood, I just stand here looking at my hands that reflect how my heart looks.

"Why are you doing this to me, Carlos, why?" I ask out loud.

By this time, I'm on the ground crying up against the tree uncontrollably. After an hour of lying there, I finally pull myself together for the trip home. When I walk into the house, I am barbate with questions from my over protecting mother.

"Baby, what happened to your hand? Does it hurt? It looks infected."

"Ma, I'll be ok, I promise. What are those?" I ask pointing at a big box in the kitchen table.

"They are addressed to a Mr. Demonte Bryant," my mother tells me.

I open the box to see the package and, as I suspected, there lay a dozen long-stemmed red roses with a note I'm saving for my room.

"They are beautiful, Honey. Who are they from?" she asks.

"The card doesn't have a name on them," I tell her.

"That's strange. Well, leave those right there and go get cleaned up cause the food is almost ready," she tells me.

"Okay," I say as I walk towards the bathroom with the biggest smile on my face and note in my hand.

When I finally wash the dry blood off and get dried off, I open the letter.

I knew he had something planned and this time he was drawing blood.

Chapter Twelve

Restart?

Somehow in some strange twisted way, Trey and I are asleep in my room by my window. I jump when I hear my alarm screaming at us and try my best to wake the hard sleeping bear beside me.

"Trey, wake up before you end up late for work," I yell at him.

"Give me twenty minutes," he mumbles.

Before I respond, I get hit with a wave of a beautiful scent of breakfast being cook.

"Aye, Mama in a good mood," I tell him.

"I'm up, I'm wide awake. Where she at, better yet where the food at?" he asks jumping up.

We go into the bathroom to wash up and make a mad dash for the kitchen table.

"Good morning, Ma," I say heading her to give her a kiss on the cheek but she walks away.

"Good morning, Demonte," she says.

I shoot Trey a look and he shoots it back.

"Morning, Ma," Trey says.

"Morning, Trey," she says.

"What's wrong with her?" I ask when I get close to him.

"I don't know," he says, shrugging his shoulders

"I can't believe she is still mad about that whole situation about me being gay," I whisper to him.

"Look, just make it through breakfast and after that, it'll be over."

"I guess."

"Look, Guys, I gotta get to work. Breakfast is on the stove and dinners in the refrigerator," she says grabbing her purse and coat and running out the door.

"Okay, that was weird. I'm to the point where I'm tired of trying to figure people out," I say.

"Something must of happened at work because her shift doesn't start until 12 and it's 10:30," my brother says.

"I just know I'm hungry," I say grabbing a plate.

"All of Me" by John Legend starts playing on my phone, letting me know that Carlos is calling me. I keep going ignoring it but somebody is more worried about it than me.

"Bra, go answer that call 'cause you know you want to," he says taking my plate out of my hand.

I go get my phone to call him back but everything is screaming do it but my heart is saying wait. I pace back and forth thinking of what should I do. But if I do call, what should I say? My phone starts ringing again and it's Carlos and I answer.

"Hello?" I say when I answer.

"Demonte, Baby, can I come see you?" he ask.

"For what?"

"You never gave me a chance to defend my name that Craig destroyed," he pleads.

"You got one minute. Go!"

"Sweetie, everything that I told you that happened that day in the car really happened. He was trying to come on to me but he wouldn't take no for an answer and that's when you came out. Baby, I swear nothing happened," he says sounding as if he is crying.

"Well explain me catching you with my ex," I say trying not to go off.

"Who?" he asks confused.

"Who else? Ryan."

"Ryan is the ex that used to bet on you?!?!"

"The one and only."

"Baby, I swear I didn't know. We are just coworkers and he came over to play the game with me. Aw, Baby, I promise you when I see him it's over," he says.

"Baby, that's in the past and that's where I'm leaving it. He's not worth your freedom or hurting yourself. What are you doing in a half hour?"

"Um, absolutely nothing. Why?"

"I'll be free around that time and I'll be willing to meet up to talk to you in person," I tell him.

I think it's time for me to forgive him because I love him and I'm starting to feel lost without him.

"Baby, thank you so much. You don't know how much this means to me," he tells me.

"Look, don't get to excited. We just meeting to talk and that's it."

"That's all I want."

"Well look, I gotta go but I will call you when I'm ready," I say before hanging up.

I walk back up front to start eating my cold breakfast. When I make it back up front, Trey is seating at the bar staring my way.

"I knew you were going to fold sooner or later," he says.

"Whatever. I didn't fold; I just wanted him to plead his case."

He just looks at me like he knows that I'm lying.

"Okay, I miss my Baby, so what? Bite me."

"I knew you were all bark and no bite young pup," he says laughing.

"What do you expect me to do? I mean at the end of the day he is still my Baby," I tell him.

I finally sit down to actually start eating my food but then my phone starts to ring letting me know that it's Carlos calling me.

"Hey, Baby. I gotta make a quick run right quick but I'll be back before you want to meet. Is that okay?" he asks.

"Yeah, Carlos. Just make sure you get back in time or else it's definitely over," I warn him in a playful voice.

"I promise to be back in time or else you can have my heart," he says.

"Too late, I already own it."

We both chuckle, but then we both get quiet. Something deep down inside is still telling me not to trust him but my heart is telling me to trust and love him.

"Look, hurry up before I change my mind. Bye."

"Bye, Demonte," he says.

Trey and I finish our food and wash the little dishes that were left in the sink.

"Trey, how you feeling?" I ask.

"I'm okay, why?"

"Trey, after what you told me yesterday, I know you're jacked up mentally. Does Mama know?"

"No, you are the only that knows. Demonte, it hurts like hell and it ain't nothing nobody can do about it, not even you. But I'll be okay because it probably not meant to be, right?"

"I guess. I just want to make sure that you are okay and that you don't do anything crazy."

"Oh, naw. You know I always keep a clear train of thought because I know you need me,' he says playfully pushing me.

"Man, whatever. I can hold this fort down with or without you."

"Are you sure about that? I mean, the way your relationship setup with Ma, I don't think that would ever happen because she is to mad at you to let you help run the house.."

"Just because Mama is mad at me does not mean I can't hold it down. Look, I gotta get ready to meet Carlos," I say leaving the sink.

"You always run when you know I'm telling the truth. But go right ahead and get to yo', Boo Boo," he says laughing.

After spending like thirty minutes picking out an outfit, I hear Tae scream out my name. I run out to the living room and see a body staggering into the front door. The person that is barely making through the door looks right at me and it is Carlos.

"Carlos! Baby, what happened?" I ask running towards him.

"Baby, I know I promised but I had to do something. I couldn't just sit back and do nothing knowing how bad he hurt you. Baby, I love you," he says trying to catch his breath.

"Baby, I told you not to do anything because I didn't want nothing like this to happen," I tell him as I help onto the couch.

I go get the peroxide, a wet, warm towel and some soap. As I walk back to the front whispering a prayer that everything is okay. When I get back to him, I see my brother trying to stop the bleeding but yet pissed that this happened.

"Trey, I love your brother and would do anything for him. I wouldn't do anything to hurt him, nothing. Everything that Craig told him are lies. You believe me don't you?" he asks not knowing that I was standing behind him.

"Yeah, I do and I'm pretty sure he does too. Just give him time to heal all of his trust issues," Trey says looking right at me.

I walk around the couch with the stuff to clean the cuts and bruises. When I touch his body with peroxide, he screams loudly and fell on his other side.

"Baby, we gotta get you to the hospital," I tell him.

"No, Baby, just clean me up and I'll be okay," he tells me in pain.

"Come on because I don't know how serious this bruises are. So, let's go," I say as me and Trey helps him to my car.

He argued with us the whole way to the car as if that would make us change our minds. When we get to the car and try to get him in to the passenger side of the car, he tries to fight us off.

"Guys, I swear, I'm fine. I just need to take a nap and I swear I'll be okay," he says.

We ignore him and I close the door in his face which muffles his plea to just 'sleep it off'.

"You wanna drive and drop me off at work on the way to the hospital?" Trey ask.

"Um, yea, I don't see why not. You better be glad yo' job is on the way or else you was go be driving your own car cause I'm in the middle of taking care of my 'Boo Boo'," I say jokingly.

We both laugh while getting on the car. The whole car is on edge and quiet except for the fact of Carlos saying that he's 'fine'. He's urking every nerve in my body and irritating my soul.

"Carlos, for the last time, SHUT UP! We going to the hospital and there's nothing you can say to change my mind. Get it, got it, GOOD!" I said.

They both just stop and look at me with shock.

"I didn't even know you had it in you," I hear Carlos mumble.

"There's nothing fine about you walking around the City of Cincinnati with infected bruises and scars."

He just sits there and just stars at me and then decides to lean over on me wrapping him on my arm. I look over at him and lay my head on top of his. It's moments like this that keeps me from staying made at him.

"Baby, I love you with all my heart. Please don't stay mad at me," he says.

I look at Trey with a devilish smile thinking to myself, 'Who won now?'

"I love you too but you go have to stop pissing me off," I tell him.

"Sir, yes, Sir."

"Well, Trey, here's your stop," I say pulling up in front of the security office.

"Thank you, Big Head. Aye, get well quick, Carlos."

"Thanks, man."

When he gets to the door, I speed off to the hospital as if somebody was chasing me there.

"Welcome to General Hospital. What happened here?" the receptionist ask wheeling a wheelchair towards us.

"He got into a little verbal altercation that turned physical. Am I right?" I ask looking down at him.

He looks at me with a puppy dog, face shaking his head "yes".

"Do we have call law enforcement?"

"No, I think this is more of a lessoned learned."

The nurse gives me a look that says she thinks I did it. I wish I was there to help cause I told his stubborn butt not to go starting trouble but what he do. He is just sits there staring at me with those big brown eyes as if he wants to say something but he just looks at me.

"Alrighty, what is the patient's name?" the nurse finally asks.

"Carlos Johnson," I answer.

"Is Cynthia Johnson your mother?" she asks Carlos.

He nods his head.

"Would you like me to page her and let her know you are being admitted?"

"Why not."

See this the attitude I'm talking about. He takes his attitude and frustration out on the people that has nothing to do with it.

"Ok, I will let her know that you are here and I will call you up when the doctor is ready," she tells us.

"See, that's why I ain't wanna come here cause I knew she work today," he says with an attitude.

"Boo hoo for the boyfriend that went against his lover's wishes and got his ass whoop. What you expect? I clearly asked and told your stubborn self not to do nothing but what you do?" I tell him with an attitude.

After sitting there for twenty minutes, his mother finally comes from where ever she came from. You can tell she is worried because of the residue of the running mascara.

"See, you got your mother nervous because of your dumb choice. Hey, Mrs. Johnson," I say as she got closer.

"Demonte, what happened? Why aren't you scratched up? I mean I'm glad to see that you are okay, but what happen to you, Boo?" she asks looking at Carlos.

"Mrs. Johnson, he found out who my abusive ex is and went to attack him. But as you can see we got this."

"Ma, please stop. I'm already in enough pain already, just spare me, please," he pleads.

"But if you had of listened to me in the first place, we wouldn't be here, now would we?" I ask him.

"Look, let me go find a doctor. Thanks, Demonte and as for you, we will talk," she says to the both of us.

"You are completely cut off. We are done, Dee. I begged you not to bring me here and what did you do," he says.

"Would you just please shut up whining you act like she wasn't go find out sooner or later. I just wanna make sure that you were okay. I just wish you would see that."

"Because Ryan said that he could have you if he really wanted you. When he said that, I just lost control and ended up at your house," he says, stopping mid-sentence.

"Stop right there because it is starting to piss me off even more," I say feeling frustrated.

I feel a tear rolling down my right cheek and his muscle bound arm wrap around me.

"Please, Babe, stop." I say pushing him off.

Just in the nick of time the doctor walks out to call Carlos back.

"Are you going back with me?" he asks giving me that puppy dog face.

"Baby, look I'll be here when you get discharged, okay?" I ask him softly.

He shakes his head and rolling his eyes.

"But just know that I really would want you back there with me though."

"I know you do but I got something to take care of," I say giving him a kiss on his bruised cheek.

"As I get to the door, I hear him softly say "Babe" and so I turned around. He mouths, "I love you". I gave him that look like "I know".

I can't wait for karma on this, I just can't. I run to the elevator as it was closing and made it. I pull my cell phone out making a conference call to Briana, Bryant, Julia and Christina to fill them in on what's going on.

Chapter Thirteen

Should I Even Care?

After the endless search for Ryan's head, I didn't get any sleep with spending the night with Carlos. I just tossed and turned all night wishing that I could just kill him to get him to leave me alone. All of my pain is coming to me as I sit a department over from mines at work writing poetry to try to relieve my bottled up stress. All of my thoughts and pain came to me as I somewhat enjoyed the view of downtown but to my surprise, I had already filled my notebook halfway.

"Hey, Demonte. I thought that was you," Alice says as she walks up behind me.

"Hey, Alice," I say covering up my notebook.

"Are you okay because you got bags," she asks.

"Yeah, I was just up studying last night and didn't get any sleep. What time is it?" I ask.

"It's 2:45," she responds.

"I'll see you in a sec, I gotta make a phone call," I tell her before I walk away.

I whip out my phone to call my Baby to see how he is feeling. The phone begins to ring but no answer which worries me the most. Then I called his house phone and still no answer. I shot Trey a text saying, "Hey is Carlos home?" After three minutes went by he finally calls me.

"It looks like he is but he is not alone," Trey tells me.

"What kinda car is it?"

"A Toyota Camry, possibly a 2005 model."

"A '05 Camry?" I whisper to myself.

"What color, Trey?" I ask him.

"Ugh, red," he tells me.

"Meet me in the foyer in ten!"

"Why, what's wrong?" he asks.

"It's wartime," I say before hanging up the phone.

I look at the time only to find out that I only have five minutes until my shift starts.

"What to do, Demonte?" I ask myself.

I finally walk over to my department looking for Gina. I go to her office that is in the back and find her there.

"Hey, Gina," I say knocking on her door.

"Hey, Demonte. What's up?" she asks.

"Um, something came up at home and I was wondering if I could leave and come back to finish my shift?" I ask nervously.

"How long do you think it will take?" she asks.

"I don't know exactly but I know it won't take long," I assure her.

"Okay, but if it takes longer than expected, I will have to consider it a call off."

"Ok, I will keep you posted," I say as I run out the door.

It really feels as if the road is a race track because I am doing at least 90 mph here. All I could think about is why is Carlos there? What part of leave me and my man alone don't get? I really don't know and I really don't care because I will fix that when I get there. When I do get home, Trey was already on the porch waiting on me.

"Bra, what's wrong?" he asks as he walks towards me.

"This little home wrecker can't take a hint and Ima end up crushing his little dream and face," I say as we walk towards Craig's front door.

All I hear is arguing as we get closer to the door and I can tell that my Baby is aggravated but that does not cover up the fact that I am mad as hell that Craig is more determined than ever to steal my man. Before I know it, I'm in the foyer smacking the living hell out of Craig.

"BABY STOP!" is all I hear Carlos say.

I could feel him and my brother trying to pull me off of him but I could tell I'm overpowering both of them.

"I'm only go say this one last time, LEAVE US THE HELL ALONE," I yell at him.

"Or else what," he mocks me.

"Look here you little incompetent bitch, the next time you bring your ass over here, you are going to need the police next time," I say staring him down.

"Sweetie, when I get done with you, you'll wish you never messed with me," Craig warns me before walking off.

I literally watch him walk out of the front door with a death stare while Carlos holds me from the back. I finally turn to him to give him a kiss which turned into a tight, long hug.

"Why, Baby? Trey, thanks man but I gotta get back to work before I end up in the unemployment line," I say as I give Craig a kiss and a hug and giving Trey a fist bump.

I whip my cell out to shot Gina a call but I see that I have a missed call from an unknown number that didn't leave a voicemail. I proceed to call Gina and the unknown called again towards the end of our phone call.

"Look, don't worry about your shift just go ahead and take care of your business because I can't deal two crazy employees right now," she tells me.

"Which employee are you referring to, Gina?" I ask her cluelessly.

"Your little friend, Craig, is having some issues and is walking around the whole department with a stupid little attitude. But I got a little for that cause I'm getting ready to fire him anyway," she continues to tell me.

"I completely understand. But look I gotta get back to my problem," I lie and say.

"Alrighty, sir. I will talk to you later, okay?"

We speak our goodbyes and I run back into Carlos' house running into my annoying brother. I went back into the house to let him a kiss, a hug and to let him know that I was not going to work.

"Hey, Baby, it's me," I say as I walk in knocking on the door.

"Hey, you," he says coming from the hallway with nothing but a pair of sweatpants and upper body covered in oil.

And people wonder why I'm in love with this sexy man. I just stand there in shock at this amazing view. We slowly walk towards with smiles in our faces.

"What are you still doing here, Baby?" he asks with a smile and a kiss.

"Well, my manager said that I can take the rest of the day off. So, I was wondering if you would like to go out for dinner and a movie after I'm down with my homework?" I ask softly.

"Baby, what if I say no?" he asks.

"But, Baby," I say giving him the Babyface and fake crying.

"Okay, I guess," he says smiling and holding me tightly.

"Gotcha," I say with a smile on my face.

He flashes me this smile makes me proud to say that I'm with him and only him. I promise you that it felt like time had stopped while I'm in his arms.

"Look, go get that homework done so we can get going because I miss you, Big Head," he says with a smile on his face.

"Ok, I guess. Give me an hour and I should be done," I tell him.

He walks me to the door like a perfect gentleman and gave me a nice firm kiss. As I was walking back towards my house I notice an all-black four-door sedan parked out front with a guy in the driver seat. It really freaked me out so I try to get a good look at the driver but I couldn't because the car was parked too far to see anything. As I got closer to the door, the feeling made my feet feel heavy like cement is forming around my ankles.

"Why ain't you at work, bra?" my brother asks as I walk through the front door.

"Yeah, but my manager told me I didn't have to come back into work," I tell him.

He shrugs his shoulders and starts to walk towards his room.

"Aye, bra. Does that black car give a funny feeling?" I ask him.

"No, why?"

"Nothing important. I just saw it on my way in and it gave off this weird vibe. But look, let me get to studying so that way I can hurry up and get to my Baby for dinner," I tell him running to my room.

As I run to my room I hear my brother making kissing sounds, so I turned and gave him the finger with a smile on my face.

"Aww, that's how you feel now?" I hear him say as I close my door.

I walk over to my bed which is covered with notebooks, textbooks and index cards to jump on top with a smile on my face. About an hour and a half into my study session, my phone vibrates letting me know that I received a text.

"Baby hurry I'm hungryyy... Wat r u trying to do starve me to death? I love you though...."

I start smiling and decide to call him.

"Baby! I hope you not trying to bail out on me," he asks answering his phone.

"Why would I do that? I really want to spend the rest of the night with that special guy, but he keeps rushing me."

"Well, are you ready now?"

"Yeah, Baby. I'm walking out the door now, so come out," I say hanging up my phone.

"Hey bra, I'm leaving out now," I tell my brother as I set the alarm.

As I walk out I see the same car from earlier parked in the same spot which seriously creeps me out. While I'm all focused on the car, I feel a warm embrace coming from the back which I know it's my annoying Baby.

"What's wrong, Baby?" he asks.

"Did you notice that car earlier when I left?" I ask him still staring at the car.

"Um, no I really didn't notice anything out of the ordinary. But then again, there are a million and one cars out here," he says pulling me towards his house.

"I guess. Look, let's go cause I'm starving and I only wanna focus on you and your smart remarks."

Chapter Fourteen

Who Can I Run To?

Well after a great night out with my Prince Charming, he melted all of those thoughts I was having about that black sedan. Sometimes I really wonder if he is somewhat stalking me or is he really my soul mate. Within this short period of time, he has helped me through so much. On our way home from our dinner I receive a text from Gina about some Halloween party and to RSVP by the 24 of October.

"Hey, Baby, wanna go to this party with me on the 31st?" I ask.

"Sure, but where?" he asks.

"At my job, I really want you to go with me, Baby."

"I'm going, Baby. What would we wear and it gotta be creative."

"How about Mr. and Mr. Johnson?" I ask looking at him hoping he doesn't say no.

He continues to look forward as if he didn't hear what I ask. I just sit here just looking at him wondering if he is embarrassed or ashamed. I grab his hand and pull it towards me.

"I'm guessing you just go ignore my suggestion?" I ask.

"Huh? I mean, yeah, Baby. Great idea. What do you wanna wear because if you going as my life partner, we gotta look extra fly?"

"I mean if you don't want to, then I'll understand," I say looking away from him.

"Look, Baby, it's not that I don't want to go, cause I do but he's going to be there."

"Baby, if you are hinting that Craig being an issue, believe me, he won't. I keep telling that you are the only one for me, do understand me?" he asks looking at me with those big brown eyes that makes me melt on the inside.

I don't know what it is about those eyes of his but I can tell that he is being honest with me. Before I knew it, I planted a nice, wet kiss on him and almost making us crash into a pole and a couple of cars.

"Babe, what the," he says gaining control of the car.

"Sorry, I mean I kinda got a little happy. I mean. I wasn't expecting a firm okay like that."

"I don't know why. I really enjoy spending time with you, I really do. You're my Baby and I don't care who knows it either," he tells me while he pulls over.

I just sat there quiet and wanting to cry so badly but I held it all in because I don't want to seem like a cry. I grabbed his hand and just sat there because honestly, I don't know how to respond to him anymore.

"Baby, I don't know what to say but I love you with all of my heart and will do anything for you. You are my heart and soul which is the reason why I get so overprotective when he comes around," I say with the biggest smile holding his hand.

He flashes me the biggest smile that makes me melt inside. He gives me a kiss on my hand and begins to pull off while holding my hand. At this point in our relationship, I don't know what to say anymore. We finally pull up to the house and as usual he gets out, comes to open my door just to walk me to my door. As usual, we walked to my door and kissed but as I turned to unlocked my door before he walks away, he grabs my arm.

"Baby, I meant every word I said in the car. I can't picture being with anybody else but you," he says to me looking me dead in the eyes.

"I know you were and I trust you with all of my being. Nothing or nobody will change that. For some reason I need you more than you think that I do so I'm going to need for you to trust me somewhere in this relationship," I tell him pulling him closer to me.

"Wanna spend the night over here with me or do you want me to come over with you?" I ask.

"It would be nice if you could come with me that way I can keep a close eye on you in my territory," he says with a huge smile as if he got something up his sleeve.

"Well, come in and help me pack then."

"What for, we're just going next door, babe?"

"To avoid coming back home later to take a shower and get a change of clothes."

"Alright, I guess but let's make it quick because I'm tired," he says rolling those beautiful brown eyes.

We finally got me things together and here comes Mr. Macho Man being noisy.

"So, where do you two love birds think y'all sneaking off to?" Treyy asks.

"Um, something you should try doing and that's minding your own business," I say.

"Alright, li'l bro. Trying to be cute in front of yo boo thang. Don't let 'em get yo ass whooped. I'm just saying homie," Treyy says.

"Aww, how cute. Trying to be Mr. Tough Guy. Stop the act Treyy cause I was just kidding."

"And I'm just saying, don't get beat up," he says walking back to his room.

"What his problem," Carlos asks.

"Who knows. He always starts acting funny when I feel like I'm replacing him," I tell him.

"Why does he fell like that? I mean I know we a couple but I'm not trying to take you away from him."

"I know you not Baby. He just has a jealous streak because I am his little brother," I assure him and giving him a kiss on the lips.

"Look, let's just go before he comes back acting like your father," he says.

He grabs my bags like the perfect gentleman as always and lets me walk out the door first.

We finally make it to his house and always smell great in here (compliments of Mrs. Johnson of course.) I absolutely got lost in the fragrance to the point that Carlos took my bags and I'm guessing to take them in his room. I hear him in the back doing something in the bathroom while I'm getting lost in the pictures in the living room. There are family photos, Baby pictures and pictures of him and his grandparents. I finally hear his footsteps coming towards the living room and then filling his nicely buff arms wrap around me. Then, he gives me a kiss up aside my head.

"You okay?" Carlos asks.

"Yeah, I'm just trying to piece together everything about and why you're the perfect guy for me. I finally see why and it's because you're a family man that was raised to be the perfect man," I tell him as I turn to face him still in his arms.

I can tell that he really appreciate what I said because he has this look in his eyes as if he wanted to start crying but he just simply gave me the biggest kiss dead on the lips. He grabs my hand and guides me to the bathroom that has a rose trial leading to the shower and ending the trail with "I Love You" in rose petals. And there are candles lit in the bathroom which looks like he had this already had this planned out.

"I really enjoyed myself tonight, Baby," I tell him.

"Well, get undress before we are both fall asleep before taking a shower because we both know how you are when you get sleepy," he says.

"And what do you mean by Mr. Johnson?"

He looks at me starts to laugh giving me a hug with a kiss on the forehead. Then we both stop to look into each other's eyes.

"You know, you make it so hard to stay mad at you with such a beautiful smile and mesmerizing eyes but not buddy boy."

"But Baby, I was just joking because you know out of all of the spoiled little brats in Cincinnati, you the only one for me because you stole my heart at first sight," he reassures me.

He gives me a smile while walks towards the shower to get the water just the way I like, nice and hot. Then he turns around to start playing the radio which Tamar Braxton's Love and War starts to play because he knows that this album is my favorite.

"Oh, don't try and redeem yourself now cause you know you done went and messed up by calling a brat and a spoiled one at that. But all of this just for me; a candle lite dinner and shower complete with playing my favorite CD. You the reason why I'm so spoiled punk."

"Can we just get in the shower, sir. I mean the water is running at the temperature you like, now hop in, NOW."

"Ok with all the rushing I might just not hop in."

"Whatever you say, boss man, whatever."

Just as we get into the shower, my favorite song comes on, Love and War and as always he sings it for because he knows how much I love to hear him singing it even though I never admitted to it.

The CD is still playing while we are drying off and "Love and War" starts to play. At that moment he grabs me in his arms and starts singing the lyrics to me to my favorite part of the song to me in my ear.

Somebody said every day, was gon' be sunny skies,

Only Marvin Gaye and lingerie, I guess somebody lies,

We started discussing it to fighting then "Don't touch

Me, please." Then it's "Let's stop the madness, just

Come and lay with me."

"The only reason why I get so mad at you is that I really care about you but you take as me nagging," I say, leading him to his room.

We both lay across his bed and he pulls me into his side, wrapping me in his arms. His phone goes off but he ignores it.

"Baby, you go get that?" I ask.

"No, it's not important," he replies still not looking at it.

It vibrates again which makes him look at it. I can tell by his body language that the person is bothering him but I lay there and say nothing,

"I'll be right back, Baby. I just gotta go to the bathroom," he says.

"Okay, but don't take too long," I say with an attitude watching him walk out the room.

When I hear him get in the bathroom, I politely grabbed his phone that was left unlocked in the message thread. Now I know that it's very shady to do this but I had to see what was so unimportant.

"OK, so I see we ain't talking any more cause of yo li'l boo thang..."

"HELLO!"

"OK, I see!"

I heard him flush the toilet so I politely put his phone back where I found it. He comes back in the room with a smile on his face.

"What's that face for?" I ask.

"Oh, nothing. Just seeing you puts a smile on my face," he replies with a sudden face change.

"But what? I know there's a but coming because your face just told me one is coming."

He looks up at me as if he wants to tell me but either he is afraid to tell me or he's afraid of how I'll take it.

"Look, Baby, you know how I feel about you. I know but I just hope that you love me as much as you say you do."

"Carlos, what's wrong?" I ask him slowly getting off the bed.

Tears start to form in his eyes. He looks away from me and lets out a big sigh. I grab his face to look him dead in his red eyes.

"Tell me, Baby."

"I, ugh, ran into Ryan the other day and he um," he says chocking on every word.

"Baby, it's okay. What he say?" I ask.

"That, um, if I don't leave you alone that he was going to do something bad to me," he says as the tears got worse.

I sat down in complete shock. I begin to cry because of the thoughts of what he did to me began to play in my head. All the pain, the abuse came back in a matter of seconds I got up and started walking to the front door.

"Baby, where are you going?!"

I keep walking not saying a word.

"Baby, stop! Where the hell are you going?" he demands.

"I'm going for a walk if that's okay with you," I respond calmly.

"I'll go with you," he says.

"No, I just need a moment alone," I tell him.

I give him a kiss, grab my jacket and leave. As I get closer to the end of the pathway, I hear a scream of frustration coming from the house, which made me start crying real bad. I grab my cell to call Julia because I really need her help to get through this.

"Hello," Julia says in a sleepy voice.

"Julia, why tonight of all nights," I say ignoring the fact that she was sleep.

"What happen?" she asks sounding fully awake.

"Well, Carlos and I were enjoying our perfect evening that he had all planned out complete with dinner, movie, a candle lite shower with roses and ended all that with a cuddle session but he told me something that messed it all up," I tell her trying to stop crying.

"What he tell you?"

"That Ryan threatens to do something to him if he didn't leave me alone."

"That bastard said what?! Demonte, what you go do? You know I don't mind popping up on people," she states.

"I know. I haven't told you the worst part. When he told me, he started to cry and from the looks of it, he was either ashamed or scared to tell me."

"Look, we'll figure out what we go do with Ryan but until then go back to Carlos and make sure that he's okay," she tells me.

"Okay, I will. Julia, thank you so much."

"Anytime Bud. Look, I'm tired but I'll see you tomorrow."

"Ok, bye."

After talking to Julia, I feel so bad for leaving him all alone. Before I go back to Carlos house, Ima just stop by my house to recoup and tell Trey what happened. When I finally get to my pathway, something keeps telling me to go to Carlos which meant something wasn't right so I ran to his. When I get to the front door, I check to see if the door is unlocked which it is. I'm hesitant to even touch the doorknob but the well-being of Carlos drives me to bust through the front door.

"Carlos, what the hell?!" I scream when I come into the living room seeing Carlos holding a .44 revolver to his head.

"Baby, I'm not man enough for you but I will always love you," he says crying his eyes out.

"Give me the gun, Baby," I say walking towards him.

"Take another step towards me, I swear I'm pulling the trigger."

I froze dead in my tracks. I'm really stuck between a rock and a hard place because I don't want him to pull the trigger but how can I stop him without moving towards him without making Carlos shot.

"Baby, I love you more than life itself but you have to give me the gun. I promise you that Ima fix this with every being of me. Please, Baby, I'm begging you," I plead walking towards him slowly.

"I don't know what I'll do without you," I tell him getting close enough to push the chamber away from his head.

"Demonte, stay aw-," he says as the chambers go off.

"Oh my gosh, Baby are you ok?" he asks dropping the gun and grabbing me.

Thank God the bullet missed me and the window.

"Yeah, Baby, I'm cool. What the hell were you thinking, Carlos?!" I ask him with tears in my eyes.

"Baby, honestly I started feeling less of a man enough when you left and then hearing Ryan saying I'm not man enough for you repeatedly in my head made it worse."

At this point, all I could do is hold him in my arms and let him cry. I've been here so many times with not only Ryan but with my father as well. At this moment in his life with this finally making him lose his sense of manhood, I don't think things will ever be the same between us, ever.

Halloween finally comes which means that the office party is today. Honestly, I don't think that Carlos is ready because I know for a fact that I know Craig will be there.

"Hey, Demonte. Is everything okay?" Gina asks.

"Hey, yeah I'm perfectly fine. I'm just a little worried about Carlos."

"Is everything okay between you two?"

"Yeah, we got into a big argument the other day and I just feel like things aren't the same between us," I tell her as I watch Carlos talk to a group of people. While I got caught watching him talk to his crew, He looks at me and flashes me a smile and I smile back. He nods for me to come to him.

"Go head to your man," she says as I look over to her for her ok.

"Off I go I guess," I say as I walk towards him with a fierce Beyoncé runway walk.

"Hey everybody, I got somebody I want you to meet," I hear him say as I get closer

"Everybody this is Demonte, the love of my life," he says as he wraps his arm around me.

"What an introduction, huh?" I whisper in his ear.

"Well, you are the one and only person that own my heart," he says giving me a kiss on the side of my forehead.

The evening is going great nut Carlos left to go to the restroom 15 minutes ago. It doesn't take that long for anybody to use the restroom especially when it's not that far. So, I decided to go find him. As I get close to the restroom, I notice a figure coming towards me which made me tense up because I know it's not Carlos.

"Hi there, Demonte," says a familiar voice.

I froze dead in my tracks because that voice hunts me until this day.

"You sick bastard," I say as I lung toward him but getting caught by Carlos' arms,

"Let me go! Just let me go," I shout as I try to fight off Carlos.

I can see that he is enjoying this little show with a smirk on his face. My adrenaline is pumping so hard that I could snap his neck with my bare hand.

"Look, fuck off you trifling bastard," Demonte says.

"Ok, I see somebody grew some grown man balls. How cute?" Ryan says while turning around laughing.

"Come near him again, there will be hell to pay," Carlos says with every muscle he has flexing.

"Whatever bitches."

Carlos turns and looks at me. I couldn't say anything just stand there, with my blood boiling with anger.

"Let's go!" I say walking away from his attempt to hug me.

Chapter Fifteen

Party Or Go Home

"Okay, Demonte, we got until one o'clock to get the ball rolling on my 22nd Birthday party," Julia says past me with her food.

"Alrighty then, let's get to planning," I say taking a bite of my burger.

"The theme colors are white and gold. I'm thinking 25 guest tops," she says looking at me for my approval.

"Ok, so we gotta plan DJ's, food, and drinks," I hear Julia say before I space out.

I hear her talking about the party, but my mind keeps retracing back to the night Carlos was trying to kill himself. Suddenly, I feel a push that knocks me out of what seems to be a daymare.

"So, you ain't even listening to me, are you?" she asks sounding annoyed.

"Sorry. What were you saying?" I ask coming back from Hellvill.

"Demonte, what's wrong?" she asks sounding really concerned.

"Um, well, you remember when I called you when I walked out on Carlos?" I ask trying to jog her memory.

"Yeah, what about it?"

"Well, I walked back into him trying to commit suicide, but ugh-," I say as my goes off.

"Hold on girl, he just texted me," I say with a smile on my face.

"This isn't working out for me… Baby, I love you, I swear but I just need time away from this, US. I will always love, Carlos."

At this point, I drop my phone on the table with tears rolling down my face.

"Demonte, what's the matter?" Julia asks.

She looks at me and then grabs my phone to read the message. Her face completely changes when she realizes why I'm crying.

"I gotta go," I say grabbing my stuff.

"Where are you going?"

"For a run."

"What about class?" she asks.

"What about it? I'll just deal with that later." I say walking away.

The pain of him breaking up with me, in a text no less kills me on the inside. The more I think about it, the harder I run to try and forget about it. Tyrese is really speaking to me right now so I decide to pump up my headphones.

How you gonna up and leave me now

How you gonna act like that

How you gonna change it up, we just

Finished makin' up

How you gonna act like that

That verse literally makes me lose it in the middle of my trail.

How you gonna up and leave me now(Why

You do)

How you gonna act like that (Why you gotta

Act like that)

How you gonna change it up (Whoa, ho,

Baby), we just

Finished making up

How you gonna act like that (But I need

You)

As I try to get the tears to stop and pull myself together, I feel a pair of muscular, smooth arms wrap around me which knocked me out of my emotional episode.

"Get off me!" I say as I look up to realize who it was.

"Baby, I'm sorry," Carlos says as he catches his balance from the push.

"Stay the hell away from me. I mean it!" I yell trying to run pass him.

"Look, Demonte, I didn't know how else to do it but that way."

"Wow and this whole time I thought I actually meant something to you. Carlos, that shit hurts and you know damn well how that would make me feel," I say but stop.

"So, that's why you did it, huh?" I ask.

"Do what?" he asks looking confused.

Before I knew it, I smacked him without thought and ran off.

I lost my train of thought so bad to the point that I didn't realize that I ran all the way to the park. Out of all the places to stop to enjoy the view, I just had to stop by the very Trey that Carlos carved our names into. I slowly trace over the carving and that's when the waterworks begin. I can't believe Carlos did this to me of all people. My music stops and I feel my phone vibrating which means that somebody is bold for calling me.

"Hello?" I answer not looking at who called.

"Oh, Demonte. How's it going?" Briana asks without speaking.

"Everything is falling apart, girl. I caught him getting ready to commit suicide but to top it all off he-," I say choking on my words fighting back tears.

"What Demonte?" she asks.

"The son of a bitch broke up with me through a text message."

We both got quiet over the phone. I can tell that we both don't know what to say, but I do know that she feels my pain because if my memory serves me right, her ex broke up with her the same exact same way.

·

"Well, what he say?" she asks finally breaking the silence.

"That he needed a break from us and that it isn't working out for him. He even swore that he still loves me," I tell her.

"Wow, that's deep. Well, can I at least cheer you up?"

"Go for it," I respond trying to sound like I was trying to cheer up.

"Well, my transfer went through and I'll be there for the next semester, but the best part is that I'm moving up there this week."

"OMG, that is some great news. I'm so happy and excited because I miss you so much. What day are you coming up?"

"I'm on the road now pushing to get to you. I'm in Nashville now fighting traffic."

"Good cause I can't wait to see you. Look, keep me posted, ok?"

"Aight, I will but let me get back to focusing on the road, ok," she says.

"Ok, bye."

"Bye."

I'm so excited that my BFF is moving to Cincinnati that it's lifting all of my pain away. All I could think about during the run back home is how much fun we'll have once she gets here. Who needs Carlos anyway?

Chapter Sixteen

Where Did I Go Wrong?

It was actually great seeing Brianna when she finally got to Cincinnati. After helping her unpack for two days, we made plans to hang out but until then I'm doing what I love to do best, writing. I'm just laying here, you know, all writing and stuff but outta nowhere I start feeling creeped out like somebody is watching me. Finally, my thirst takes over, so I decided to take a drink of water.

"What the hell, Trey," I say almost knocking my bottle of water over.

"My bad, li'l bro. I was just thinking" he says walking towards my bed.

"About?" I ask making room for him on my bed.

"A lot, Demonte. It's just a lot going through my mind, man."

At this point I feel like I haven't been there too much for him like I have in the past. But I'm here now right?

"What's wrong, Tre?" I ask as if I was annoyed.

"Look, you're my little brother and you know I love you more than anything," he says.

"Here we go with that 'I love you' bs," I say taking a deep breath.

"Look, you're my little brother and nothing is go change that but I gotta admit something to you," he says looking at my bedroom door.

I sat up looking at him with a look of confusion because I clearly don't know what he's hinting around.

"I just can't accept the fact that you gay, man. I tried but the more I think about it, it just doesn't sit well with me."

When he said that, it felt like I was hit by a bus. At this point, I'm all cried out and I can't find the tears or the words for this situation. I get up, grab my keys and jacket heading to the door.

"Demonte, I'm sorry bro," he says chasing me.

"Trey, leave me alone. I can't with you or anybody else. Out of all people, I thought yo' ass actually had my back. You ain't shit, bra but a fake ass that don't give a damn about me nor my damn feeling's," I yell while grabbing my things to walk out the door. I got in my car and started to drive without a destination in mind. For some reason, I end up on Brianna's street creeping up to her apartment building when I finally come to. Thankfully, she is already outside doing God knows what.

"What's up Demonte?" she asks when she gets to the passenger side window.

"Get in, just get in," I lightly whisper.

She gets in full of fear and I pull off not knowing our destination. When I finally park, I realize that we are at Eden Park by the spot of Carlos and I first date. With a numb heart like mines, it's hard to feel any type of emotion.

"Demonte, what's up? You haven't said a word since I been in the car," she says.

I can tell that she is worried and that the way that I'm acting is scaring her. I wouldn't even know where to start.

"When all else fails, your brother, your only brother is telling me that he doesn't agree with your 'lifestyle'."

"Why does your brother gotta be an asshole and cute at the same time?" she asks shaking her head.

"You telling me. I mean he sits up here telling me that he supports me but pulls stunts like this. It's as if he doesn't care how I fell. Doesn't he know how much this killing me on the inside?" I say as I feel the tears roll down my cheeks.

We literally sat in my car for hours crying and staring at the view of Kentucky and the river. I literally toss and turn all night long not getting a second of sleep. The thoughts of what happened between Tre and me replayed over and over in my mind. At this point in my life, I'm all cried out with nothing to say to anybody. I moved very slowly getting ready for class because I lack the energy to move any faster. I barely said two words to words to Trey (even though he spoke as if nothing ever happened) and I barely talk to anybody at school including Julia. As we both walk to class, it's a long and cold walk there. Usually, we're able to seat together but today for some reason, it's super crowded.

"We'll talk later, okay?" she says taping my shoulder as she went to take a seat that she found.

All I could do is stand there even though there is a seat clearly empty in front of me.

"Have a seat, Mr. Bryant and see me after class," Mr. Lee says as he enters the room behind me.

I cringe, closing my eyes to say a little prayer walking towards the empty sit.

"Good morning, class. Today we'll be discussing the final exam and term paper. The final paper is worth 25% of your grade as well as the final exam will be worth 50%," he says as I begin to slowly black out.

At this point, I don't know what's going on in class but I do know that my so-called brother is blowing up my phone. I kinda tune into class just in time to hear Mr. Lee wrapping up class, which I'm all too glad about.

"So, do we understand what will be going on for the next couple weeks?" he asks.

We all answer in agreement even though I can't tell you what will even be going on net class. Everybody begins to grab their things as he dismisses class and I try sneaking out which is an obvious fail.

"Mr. Bryant, have a minute?" he asks grabbing me with the authority in his voice.

"Yes sir," I say stopping mid-step with an attitude written all over my face.

"Demonte, I've noticed a tremendous drop in your grades the last few weeks. Is everything okay?" he asks.

"Yeah, I'm good just been a little busy at work that's all," I say trying to maintain my attitude.

"I'm more than willing to help you pass this class but I-,"

"Look, I said I got this. I'm good, I don't need any help. I'M PERFECTLY FINE!" I scream, running to the door.

Before I knew it, I slam the door behind me, running with no destination in mind. Before I know it, I find myself outside the cafeteria in the middle of the grass overlooking the expressway and train terminal.

"What am I doing wrong with my life?" I ask myself quietly with tears rolling down my cheeks.

I feel my phone vibrating; I reach in for it but knocking a small bottle out with it. I bend over to get the bottle that seems to be a pill bottle completely ignoring the call. Realizing that it's enough pills to carry out my little plan. I dash to my car to get home to carry it out. When I get home, I'm greeted by my mother.

"Hey, Demonte. How was school?" she asks.

Before I could answer, I'm then greeted by the floor and then hearing my mother scream for me.

Chapter Seventeen

Rocky Road To Recovery

I'm still alive and I'm in the hospital. Ok, now I'm starting to feel a little more and it's starting to feel like I'm in a super small bed under some comfortable blankets. Now that I'm getting all of my functions back, I hear a female crying. And why does it feel like somebody is holding my hand with a pair of oversized bear claws? Hell, that means that Carlos and my mother is here for sure. I try to open my eyes just a little bit to see who's here but instead my fingers decide to twitch alerting Carlos.

"Baby, are you with me?" I hear Carlos ask.

"Doctor, he's moving!" I hear my mother shout.

"Ow, not so loud guys," I moan when a headache finally hits me hard.

"Ok, everyone, I need some room," I hear from a guy in a white jacket.

"Demonte, I'm Dr. Biermann. Can you tell me your full name?" he asks.

"Demonte Durrell Bryant," I answered annoyed.

"When is your birthday?" he asks while flashing a bright light in my eye.

"March 26, 1993," I answer slightly confused.

Why did I have to think that answer up? Did I suffer memory loss with that fall?

"Try something a little harder like when is your mother's birthday?" I hear my brother ask from behind the doctor.

"November 10th, why?" I ask sarcastically.

"He's back," Julia and Brianna chime in laughing.

"Everything looks good. I just wanna keep him for the next few days for observation and start some counseling sessions. Ok, Demonte?" he asks before leaving the room.

"Just great. This is what I need right before the best party of my life," I reply with an attitude.

"Seriously, Demonte? You just tried to take your own life and you worried about some party?" my mother yells.

Before I know it, everybody heads for the door, leaving the helpless, weak, gay guy to defend for himself.

"What were you thinking? Why would you want to take your own life?" she asks with a tear rolling down her face.

"Mom, honestly, I wasn't thinking at all. The only thing that I think about was ending my life. I just don't know why I did it," I tell her holding back tears.

"But why didn't you come talk to me about this, about what was bothering you?"

"Ma, that's the thing. I'm bothered by the way that you and Trey have been treating me since I came out. I'm bothered by how I haven't felt comfortable in my own home since then. At this point, are we really a family?"

By the look on her face, I can tell that I really just hurt her with the truth. Before I could say anything, she gets up and walks out the door.

"Ma, wait. Don't leave!" I call out to her.

She stops in her tracks at the door and shakes her head walking out. After about a good minute, my door opens back but it's not my mother.

"Hey, guys," I say as I see Trey, Carlos, Julia and Brianna walk in.

"What you say to Ma, cause she left here pissed and didn't say anything to me," my inconsiderate brother ask.

"Well, we talked about why I'm here," I respond nicely as I possibly know how.

"Now, why the hell are we here cause I ain't got time for your smart remarks?" he replies.

I tense up as all of their eyes all beam at me as if they're staring into my soul for the answer.

"Ugh, didn't Mom or the doctor tell you what happened?"

"Obviously not if I'm asking you," Trey says sarcastically.

"Demonte, look, just be honest and cut the bull. What really happened?" Carlos asks trying to keep his cool.

As I look around the room, the confusion in their eyes is screaming 'tell us the truth' but I really can't get myself to do that. How do you tell somebody that you wanted out on life?

"Um, well guys, I really don't know how to say this but I ugh," I say trying to find the words to tell them.

"Baby, please, just say it," Carlos whispers to me with a cracking voice.

"I tried to commit suicide," I blurted out.

Brianna stares at me in shock, Julia turns towards the door, Carlos buries his face into my hand covering them in tears and Trey walks out my room slamming the door behind him.

"We'll go check on him," Julia says looking towards Brianna.

"Baby, I'm sorry," Carlos says looking at me with a wet face.

When our eyes connect, I see that he really feels like he's responsible. In a way, the events that happened between us do play a part in why I tried to do it.

"Carlos, honestly, I feel like one minute you care and the next it's all about you. At this point, I don't know if I love you or love you the same. I feel like we just need to continue this break with no communication," I say, choking on the last words.

He looks at me as if I said something wrong or out the blue. We are on break and I don't want any communication during this time. Then he's giving me this surprised look.

"Baby, you don't mean that, do you?" he says with a fresh batch of tears flowing.

"Did you say that when you the one that broke up with me through a text message? Do you know how that killed me emotionally?"

Before he could respond, my door swings open with a ragging Trey coming through it.

"Do you know the hell that you could have put us through?! Why are you so damn selfish?!" he yells out.

"Mr. Bryant, is everything okay?" a nurse asks through the speaker.

"Can you please have security come escort everyone out of my room? Please," I answer.

"Oh, so now when I step to you man to man, you wanna have me and everyone else kicked out?" Trey asks with an attitude.

"Trey, it's a little too late for your concern."

"Oh, Trey you ain't the only one that he's lashing out on. Let your brother tell it, I'm the most heartless guy in the world," Carlos responds.

"But, Demonte, why us?" Brianna asks as she and Julia take a seat close to me.

"Guys, despite what these two jerks have to say, I just need this time to recover," I tell Brianna and Julia very patiently.

"You know what, we out. My own blood is kicking me of all people out," Trey says as him and Carlos walks toward the door.

"And it's funny how my own blood turns they back on me when my sexuality changes."

"Look, we understand if you need this time alone; we get it. But don't forget, we are one phone call away," Brianna says as they take turns giving me a kiss goodbye.

I can't believe that this is happening me; I can't that I didn't get the help that I needed. I let things build up for so long that I didn't think clearly. My life is a mess because I didn't speak sooner. On the other hand, I can't believe that my family didn't have my back when I needed them the most. Then, on yet another hand, there's Carlos. The guy I thought was the man of my dreams, the love of my life. He was shallow enough to sit up here and break up with me via text message. I really don't know where I am right now in my life because my mind is so cloudy and I feel like I can't see straight. Am I losing sight of who I really am? I don't know but I will get back on the right track.

"Nurse," I say as she chimes in on the speaker. "I would like to place my mother, Joy Bryant, my brother, Trey Bryant, my ex-boyfriend, Carlos Johnson and my friends, Julia and Brianna on my list of 'No Call and Visit' list."

"Anybody else?" she asks.

"That'll be all," I answer.

"Ok, I will let the head of security and front desk know," she says as she disconnects.

As I lay in an empty room, lonely as possible, I can just feel the emptiness, the pain, the confusion all just hit me all at once with the batch of tears coming. Why me? A knock at the door startled me up from my sleep and from the looks of it, I cried myself to sleep because the sun was going down not rising.

"Demonte, it's Reverend Jackson," I hear a familiar voice call from behind the curtain.

"Hey, Reverend, come on in," I call out when I gain conciseness.

"How are you feeling today," he asks.

"I'm great, I really am," I answer knowing that we both know that I'm lying.

"I heard why you are here, so tell me how you feeling," he responds to my lie.

"Pastor, honestly I don't know why I did it. I just couldn't handle the pressure anymore. I just wanted the quickest way out," I tell him the partial truth.

"Well, from what I heard, and I'm not the one to listen to the words of others mouth, but the reason is the fact that you are gay. Is that true son?" he asks looking me dead in the eyes.

Wait, wait! Did my aunt sell me out to the Pastor? Or was it my mama? I know she's made but to sell me out to the Pastor? But I bet it was Trey. Naw, Trey don't even tell his sins so why tell mines? I can't catch a break.

"Well, Pastor, you had it right, you shouldn't listen to gossip, especially from lonely, bitter old women with nothing better to do with their lives but spread lies about everybody else. No disrespect, but I just don't like discussing my personal business," I say looking him dead in the eyes. "But I will tell you this, I am gay but I don't feel the need to broadcast it all over the place."

"Well, I see your point, but you do know the Bible says in Leviticus 18:22, 'Thou shalt not lie with mankind as in womankind: it is abomination.' Son, as the Pastor over you, I'm just trying to keep your soul from an eternity in hell," he tells me with compassion in his eyes.

A part of me wants to go off, but another part knows he is right. At this point, I don't know if I should hold back my emotion or should I just let it all out? He is my Pastor and I know I should talk to him with respect, but for some reason, I don't feel the respect from him. I'm just all messed up.

"Look, Pastor, no disrespect but I just don't feel comfortable talking about my personal life," I say looking him dead in the eyes, "especially when the information is coming from my miserable family."

"I completely understand your frustration but the only way to get through this letting go of the sin, seek God and let Him lead you."

I don't know if the meds are still in my system or what, but my attitude and my patients are super thin right now. I try to hold my tongue, or what's left of it, but I can't sit here and be chastised in such a manner. But just as I am about to say something a knock on the door saves him.

"Sorry to interrupt but visiting hours are up and Mr. Bryant, you need to get some rest because you have a busy day ahead of you," the nurse says coming in to check my monitor.

The pastor looks at me with a look of despair and disbelief but he gathers his things to leave. As he approaches the door he turns to look at me one last time.

"Demonte, no matter what happens, just know that God and I love you," he says walking out the door.

As the nurse checks my vitals, all these questions pour into my head. While I continue to ponder, my heart monitor starts to beep loudly. Is God trying to take me out early?

"Calm down, Mr. Bryant. Are you feeling ok?" she asks.

"Yeah, I'm ok. It's just family issues that got me a little bothered," I respond breathing in and out.

"Well, it's not good to have your heart racing this fast. It could lead to a heart attack or even a stroke," she responds, "but everything looks great."

"Good, good. I just want a healthy, speedy recovery."

"And that's what we want for you, but mental health is a very quiet thing in the Black community. I just wish this and other stereotypes would end, especially with the saying, 'When men talk about their problems, it's a sign of weakness.' That may be true but if talking it may save a life, I'm all for a man showing his vulnerable side."

As I lay here, all I can do is think how right she is. While she is finishing up, my mind, body and soul keep thinking and wanting Carlos. I don't know why I'm beyond angry with him. My mind continues to go back to the night he planned the most romantic night with the rose petal trail leading to the shower.

"Alright, I'm all done. If you need anything else, give us a call," my nurse says knocking me out of my daydream.

"There's one thing; everybody who was here today, I think it'll be best not to see them for couple days."

"Are you sure?" she asks.

"Yeah, I'm pretty sure. I just need a few days to clear my head."

"I'll make sure everyone gets the memo," she says as she leaves the room.

I check my emails for the umpteenth time, not knowing what I'm looking for. As I lay here, I try to figure out my life from here and all I can think about is poetry. Grabbing my notebook, I feel the words flowing through me as if my soul had something to say but I can also feel myself drifting off.

A knock on the door disturbs my uncomfortable sleep.

"Come in," I respond after realizing that I'm still stuck in this hell hole.

"Good morning, Demonte. My name is Dr. Thomas and I'll be working with as your psychiatrist for the next few days," a tall mocha man in an all-white lab coat says as he approaches the side of my bed with a stool.

As he sits down, I can't help but give him the blankest stare; without any expression whatsoever. Honestly, I don't know why I give people the hardest time, but I can't help myself.

"How's your day going so far?" he asks.

"It's a going," I reply unenthusiastically.

He gives me this look that says, 'I don't have time for your smart remarks.' Honestly, I could care less. After everything that has happened, how can I care about anything at all?

"Do you understand why I'm here?" he asks.

"Do I understand why you are here? Do you understand why I'm here? I have a family that hates me, a brother that can't stand my sexuality, I have a delusional ex that won't leave me alone with a boyfriend and a group of friends that hate me because I tried to kill myself," I rush out with tears in my eyes.

"Anything else?" he asks quietly unsure of another episode.

"Oh yeah, and a boyfriend that ain't even sure that he wants me."

At this point, the doctor is looking at me like I'm crazy but he wanted to know.

"Ok, so tell me how this makes you feel."

Once again, he gets the blank stare.

"Do my tears not tell you nothing? I'm in pain, I'm angry, I'm upset! I've been having these same set of emotions run through me since before I tried to kill myself."

After releasing the tension, my phone vibrates letting me know that I have a new text message. As bad as I want to open it, I just ignore it. While I watch the doctor take notes, my phone vibrates again but this time it's a call.

"So, Demonte, tell me a little about your childhood," the Doctors says not looking up from his notepad.

As the question constantly replays in my head, I don't even know where to start. Do I start at the beginning? Do I start where my pain began? At what point and time does he want me to start?

"Demonte, are you still with me?" he asks.

"Oh, I'm sorry. What was the question?" I ask playing it off.

"Let's talk about your past so I can better help your future."

"Well, um, I was born here back when it was 'General Hospital'. There's really nothing to tell besides the fact that we moved to Birmingham, Alabama when I was five and then we just recently moved back so I can attend UC. I live a pretty dull life."

I honestly can't even relive what I went through verbally. I can't stomach the thought of how I was verbally, physically and sexually abused. No one really don't know how it feels to suffer the way I, my brother and my mother did.

"Did you grow up with just your mother and brother? Was your father even in the picture?"

"Ugh, my father was in the picture until his death from a drug overdose."

"My condolences. How did that make you feel?"

"A lot of emotions," I tell him.

He looks up from his notepad with a confused but a concerned face. He acts like just because the father was in the picture, everything is peaches and cream. I mean, yeah everybody story is different, but mines involve all types of abuse. All of which I'm not willing to discuss I might add.

"Do you care to elaborate?" he finally asks.

I feel my eyes roll with an attitude. "Sure," I say as I try to stay positive.

"My father was abusive towards my brother, mother and I until his death. Then after years of abuse from him, I met my abusive ex-boyfriend, Ryan," I tell him looking straight ahead.

"As you can see, I have a marvelous history with abuse," I say as he continues to write in his pad.

"What type of abuse did you endure with your father and this ex of yours?" he asks.

"They were both verbal and physical."

It gets very quiet and uncomfortable but then his pager goes off. Thank God!

"Well Demonte, we have gotten a lot of things covered today. Throughout your duration here at the hospital, we will have daily meetings to help better your mental state. How about tomorrow around 10:30?" he asks.

"I'll be here. I'm pretty sure I'm not anywhere else, Doc."

"Alrighty, see you then," he says as he exits.

My phone vibrates again and it's a call from Carlos.

"What do you want?" I ask, answering the phone.

"Why are you torturing me?" he asks.

I can tell by the tone in his voice that this suicide mission that it's taking a toll on him.

"I swear, I love you!"

"You have a very funny way of showing it, Carlos."

"Demonte, forget the text, forget the petty arguments, forget every negative thing that has been brought up in this relationship."

It feels like time has frozen when hearing this. All this time, I've felt alone. True enough that Carlos brought this guilt upon himself when he sent that text, but I can tell that he genuinely loves me.

"Baby, are you there?" he asks.

"Yeah, I'm here. Do you mean everything you just said?" I ask with too much enthusiasm.

"Would I have said it if I didn't?"

"Don't be mad, but I just need some time to clear my mind, ok?"

He gets quiet for a second which scares me.

"Demonte, love is kind and love is patient. Take all the time you need."

"Thank you. Look, I gotta go but I love you, too."

"I know and I love you too. I'll talk to you later," he says as we hang up.

He honestly knows how to make me smile, how to make me cry, how to make me how to make, make me feel in love. Could this be love? Is this love? As I lay here, all I can think about is if Carlos is the one.

"Good morning, Demonte!" a familiar voice says waking me up out of my sleep.

"Y'all go learn that, one, I'm not a happy morning person and two, I'm an even more of an unhappy person when I'm woken up out of my sleep," I say finally focusing on the familiar voice.

"Sorry to intrude, especially at this hour. I just wanted to get our session started at a decent hour if that's okay with you?"

"Sure, why not?" I reply propping myself up.

"Well, we have been communicating for almost a week and I think you're almost ready for the outpatient part of your treatment after a couple more inpatient sessions," he says looking over his notes.

"Sounds excellent to me," I say finally perking up.

After exactly one whole hour, my session is finally over. Thinking back on all of my sessions, I think it's really time for me to start forgiving everybody starting with Carlos. I grab my cell to send him the message to come to the hospital around three, sent my brother and mother the same message telling them to be here at 4 and sent Julia and Brianna a 5 o'clock appointment. After seeing their response, it makes me feel wanted and valued.

For a while, it seemed like the only best friend I had was my notebook. Like now, I'm buried in my notebook to the point where I don't realize that it's 3 and the fact that Carlos is standing at the foot of my bed calling my name.

"I see that some things haven't changed in a good way," he says grabbing with a smile taking my notebook and pen.

"Hey, my bad. How was work?" I ask, leaning up for a kiss.

"It was cool, I guess. Baby," he says, grabbing my hand looking down at the floor.

"Wassup?"

"Baby, I've been doing a lot of thinking during our time apart but just know that I really do love you."

All I can do is grip his hand harder with a smile on my face.

"Baby, I know you do. That's why I asked you to come here. I asked you here to tell you that I forgive you. I forgive you enough to start over with you but this time a little slower."

"Demonte, are you serious?" he asks looking up at me with a wet face and a smile.

"Yes, I'm serious and sure. Things have been rough, but things have also been good. I honestly can see a bright future with you. You have been there for me through a really rough spot in my life and I truly appreciate and love you for that."

We both start crying at this point. He gives me the tightest hug and cuddles me in this tight bed. We lay in my bed until my mother and brother come and after that time, time just flies by until I've had my one on one time with everybody.

"Look, y'all, I appreciate everybody showed up but a brother is tired. Y'all know people don't sleep in a hospital," I say with a faint smile.

"Aight, I guess," my brother says leaning in for a hug.

"Look, when you get out of here, I promise everything will be better," my mother promises while giving me a hug and a kiss.

My girls give me a hug and a kiss, and Carlos stands there smiling like he ain't about to bounce with 'em.

"Aight Carlos, lay it on me so you can go too," I say prepping for a kiss.

He stops and looks down as if he's not ready.

"Look, you ain't gotta go home, but gotta get up outta this room," I say playfully.

"I know and I am, I just love you so much, Demonte. I don't know what I'd do if I really lost you this time."

"Oh, look at my baby being all sentimental," I say trying to lighten up the mood.

"Demonte, I'm not joking right now with you."

"I know, I know. At this point, we all know that I was in a really bad place in my life. Baby, I really do love you and wouldn't do anything to intentionally hurt you," I say holding his cheek.

We have an awkward silence for a moment before he lays a long, warm kiss on me. While he walks out, he almost runs into my nurse, who's wearing all white, almost knocking my diet, dark drink all over her. I try not to laugh but he makes accidents like these look cute. I can feel the love from him but it feels different this time. Different as in I have can tell that I have his whole heart, body and soul; real love and nothing less. With sleeping in this extra small hospital bed ain't too bad after all.

Just like clockwork, Dr. Thomas knocks on my door, we have our session but this session feels different than our other ones.

"So, I have some great news, Demonte," he says looking up at me with a smile.

"What's up, Doc?" I ask all concerned

"From the looks of it, I'll be discharging you today."

I can feel all my excitement rush straight to my face. "Really, Doc?" I say wanting to cry from joy.

"Yes, Demonte. I already filled out the paperwork but I wanted to have one last session before I submitted them to see your state of mind first," he says packing up to leave.

"If there's nothing else, here's my card if and when you are ready to start sessions outside of this room," he says handing me his card. "It was a pleasure meeting you, Demonte," he says before opening the door.

"Doc," I call out catching him before he walks out, "Thank you so much."

"Anything for my favorite patient," he says with a smile.

Chapter Eighteen

A Different Us

It feels wonderful to be on this side of the hospital walls but, for some reason, it feels funny at first being back into society. However, it's also the beginning of a new start. The only person that knows of my discharge is Carlos and our first stop is the mall.

"Surprise," a familiar voice says as a bouquet of long stem roses appears in front of me.

"Well, what a beautiful surprise, Mr. Bouquet," I say turning to greet him with a smile and a kiss.

"Anything for the best thing that ever happened to me," he says with the biggest smile on his face.

"Oh, wow! That's a new one."

"Well, it took me almost losing you to realize but it's the true baby," he says trying to convince me.

"Look, I'm ready to shop. You buying, right?" I ask with a serious tone.

"Of course, Babe," he tells me pulling me through the mall.

"So, how's it going with counseling?" Carlos asks as I decide what store to get to first.

"Everything is great. The Doctors are saying that I'm making a great comeback. Let's go in here," I say finally finding my favorite store.

"That's great. So, what's up with us?" he asks quietly.

"As far as what?" I ask with one brow raised.

"As in a couple."

"Wait, pause. Let me cut this confusion short. What we 'had' is like a mirror; if you shatter it, it cracks and breaks, right?"

"Right," he asks confused.

"Well, you can put the pieces back together but the cracks will still be there. So, while I try this on, I want to think about it."

I can tell by his facial expression that he doesn't. I love him to pieces but the trust isn't there anymore and I feel like he's scared of commitment.

"Okay, I like them all. So, that means that I'll just have to half on it with you," I tell him with an armful of clothes.

"Well, technically, I said I was doing all of the buying, remember?" he says with a devilish grin.

"Mama ain't raise no dummy. She always said, 'When somebody opens up their whole wallet to you, take it all,'" I say with a lot of strength behind it.

"Anything to see my baby happy again," he says.

"As we grab my clothes, he takes my hand while looking me dead in my eyes as if he wants to tell me something but holds it back.

"So, what do you have the taste for besides draining my bank account?" he says smirking.

"See, that's what I'm talking about. I clearly told you that I would go in on half of the total," I say trying to sound really hurt.

"I'm just playing, Babe. But what do you really want to eat?"

"Um, how about pizza?"

He gives me this look as if he's highly upset that I said pizza.

"What? You too good for pizza now?" I ask in a serious voice.

"No, it's just I kinda ate pizza the last three night's in a row," he says as if he's nervous to tell me.

"Okay, how about Chinese food?"

"The usual?"

"With extra Lo Mein and chicken," I tell him with a kiss before heading to grab a seat.

For some reason, I start getting this weird vibe like somebody's watching me.

"One large diet, General Tso with extra Lo Mein and chicken," I faintly hear Carlos say. I hear him talking but I can't help but case the food court.

"Bae, Bae!" I hear him call out while pushing me.

"What? What's wrong?" I ask.

"Question is what's up with you?"

"Ugh, nothing I just got this weird vibe like somebody is watching me or us for that matter."

"You're probably just paranoid. Look, you're with me now so you have nothing to worry about. Is that okay with you?" he states as he caresses my check.

"You know it is. That's why it hurts when you pull those stunts because I, I ugh," I say starting to lose my train of thought.

"What is it?"

"Carlos, I love you so much that it hurts. You are actually the first guy that I can honestly be myself with and actually feel safe with."

I guess I dropped a bomb because he just looks down. Was it something I said? Was I to brutally honest? I don't know, I just don't.

"I know this, Demonte. Since we're being honest, I gotta get this off my chest. I'm nervous that you may use my love as a weakness and use it to your advantage. But," he says.

"But what? But you feel bad about what happened so that's why you staying? But what Carlos, what?"

"But I see that you genuinely love me. You show me unconditional love which is something I'm not used to getting from another man."

"Oh, sorry. My bad, Baby," I say embarrassed that I completely went off for no reason.

"It's cool because I completely understand why you are on edge. After what I did, I wouldn't trust me either. You ready to go, though?"

"Yeah, just let me go get a refill," I tell him while grabbing my cup.

"Aye," Carlos calls out.

"What?"

"Don't take too long," he says with a huge smile on his face.

The walk to the car is awkwardly quiet.

"You staying over, right?" he asks finally breaking the silence.

"Yeah, I guess."

Once again, the atmosphere grows quiet between us. But I do know one thing, what Carlos said earlier really got me thinking a lot. The fact that he thinks that I don't trust him is somewhat true. If I'm honest with myself, I really don't. As we hold hands, I can feel him shack.

"Are you nervous about something?" I ask gripping his hand harder.

"No, no. Everything is perfectly fine," he says as he kisses my hand.

"Okay, well let me run this in the house and I'll be right over," I tell him as he pulls into his driveway.

To my surprise, everybody in my house is asleep. I honestly don't know how to face them at this point. Even though we were on better terms at the hospital, I still feel like something is broken between us.

"Demonte?" Trey calls out.

"Not so loud, I don't need you waking Ma up," I say quietly.

"My bad. When did you get discharged?" he asks as we give each other a hug.

"Around 2 o'clock-ish. I would've called but I just wanted some alone time. Plus, Carlos wanted to take me out."

"I get it. What are you doing tomorrow?"

"Oh, I don't know yet because I'm spending the night at Carlos' house. Why?"

"I might actually want to take you out to breakfast. Just let me know."

"Ok, I will. Now go back to bed," I say trying to cut it short with him.

"Aight, I am. Be safe," he says walking to his room.

"Carlos, where you at?" I call out as I walk through the front door.

"My room, baby," he says.

"So, what's this?" I ask.

He has scented candles, long-stemmed red roses and a bowl of popcorn on the bed.

"Well Baby, we going to watch your favorite movie."

"You've got mail?" I ask joyously.

"You know it!"

"Hurry up and press play."

"Okay, okay."

"Thank you for this. You don't know how much this means to me."

"I can tell by the look on your face that it means a lot to you. Now shhh! The movie is starting," he says, wrapping his arm around me.

As I look at Carlos, there is just something about him that makes it somewhat worth it. But as I look at him tonight, right now, I sense a certain glow about him like he finally gets my pain but also wants to fix the problem. I can tell that he's genuinely happy to be with me. My phone vibrates, completely ruining the romantic mood, letting me know that I have a text message.

"We still on?"

"Ain't u supposed 2 b sleep?" I reply.

"Such the smart mouth… U going or not?"

"OMG YES! What time?"

"10?"

"Ok see u at 10… Peace out!"

"Deuces."

"Who's texting you this late?" he asks half sleep.

"My brother. He wants to take me out to breakfast. Did you have any plans for us already?"

"Yeah, but it can wait till later."

"You sure?"

"Yeah, I'm sure."

"Okay, so what're the big plans for tomorrow?"

"You'll see."

"But, baby, I need to be wardrobe ready,"

"Just wear something simple."

"I guess. So, how's school coming along?"

"It's coming along great. I passed my exams."

"Thanks, Baby. Come here," he says pulling me closer to him.

Ring the alarm, I been through this too long.

But I'll be damned if I see another…

"Hello," I answer with a dazed voice.

"Bro, where are you?" Trey yells into the phone.

"Oh my gosh! What time is it?" I ask finally waking up.

"11:30. And Mama said you come say 'Hi' before she goes to work."

"Look, give me five minutes and I'll be over," I say, quietly trying to get dressed without waking Carlos.

"Aight."

"Hey, Ms. Linda," I say as I approach her when I finally make it to the front.

"Hey, Baby. How are you feeling?" she asks as she gives me a kiss.

"I'm better than I was a week ago. How've you been?"

"I've been great just been busy at the hospital. Is my knucklehead son still sleeping?"

"Yes, Ma'am. Speaking of which, can you please let him know that I'll be ready in an hour?"

"I sure will. Have a good day, baby," says walking back into the kitchen.

"You too," I say running out the door.

"Look who decides to show up," Trey says as I make my way across the yard.

"So, when were you going to tell me you were home. Oh, I mean at Carlos house?" my mother asks.

"Like always, Trey leaves at the important parts," I say as I give her a hug and a kiss.

"I guess, Demonte. If you boys get hungry later, there are leftovers in the fridge. I'm working late and I'm running late. See you guys later," she says hopping in her car.

"Bye, Ma," we both say in unison.

"Okay, where we going cause you paying?" I ask ready to get this little date over.

"Well, what's the rush?" he asks frowning at me.

"If you gotta know, Carlos actually wants to take me out for lunch. Is that a problem?"

"Kinda, I was trying to spend the day with you. But I get it, you wanna spend time with your man," he says sounding hurt.

"Look, man or not, you know I'm down to spend time with you. I'll just call and reschedule," I say trying to compromise.

"Look, just enjoy brunch and a movie with me and I'll be satisfied. Cool?"

"Cool."

So, he decides to take me to my favorite brunch restaurant: First Watch. I place my usual but Trey, as always, is being difficult.

"Trey, why can't we ever go somewhere without you being difficult?" I ask lightweight pissed.

"I mean I have a certain way I like my food cooked," he says looking confused.

"Man, messing around with me, you'd go hungry with all yo' demands," I say with a full-blown attitude.

"Here we go with the attitude. You are super sensitive."

"I'm just saying, you ain't gotta be that difficult when we get in public."

"You right, I can't even lie. But if I'm paying for it, why not get it the way I want it?"

I got to admit, even though he gets on my nerves, he got a point. Before I get an opportunity to say something, our food finally comes.

"Thank you," I say as the waitress finish putting the food on the table.

As usual, the table grows quite due to the fact that we are too occupied with food to talk.

"Okay, so what movie do you wanna go see?" he asks taking a sip of his orange juice.

"Honestly, I just wanna see Carlos," I say.

"Okay, so where to?"

"Let me ask," I say as I grab my cell phone.

"Where r u?!"

"Just left the house... Meet me at the cut in the park with the view... TTYL bout to drive..."

"Okay, he wants to meet in the park where we had our first date. I wonder what how's up to."

"Well, let me go pay. Meet you at the car?" he asks as he grabs his stuff.

"Yeah."

During the whole ride, there's a lot of things are going through my mind. I'm quite shocked that my brother ain't put up a fight for my attention. I could be tripping, but I feel like these two are up to something. As we get closer to the meeting place I see Carlos' car with Carlos leaning on the back of his car.

"Wassup, homie," my brother greets Carlos when we pull up near him.

"Nothing much, just maintaining and trying to survive college. 'Sup with you?" he asks while opening my door.

"Same thing minus the school part. Look, I gotta jet but y'all enjoy y'all selves."

"Peace out, home slice," I say grabbing Carlos' arm.

"Aight Trey."

While Trey pulls off, Carlos leads me to this picnic that resembles the same one from our first date. This picnic is complete with my favorite pastries and cake.

"Well, considering you already ate, I went to your favorite bundt cake shop and got a red velvet cake and a white chocolate mocha cake complete with your favorite cookies and blueberry muffins," he says presenting me the spread compete with an orchid in the middle.

"Oh, Baby, I love it," I say giving him a kiss on the lips.

"Have a seat."

"Don't mind if I do."

"How was your day so far?" he asks passing me a slice of red velvet cake,

"It was cool. Trey wanted to go see a movie but I just wanted to see my man."

"Aww, look at you, being all romantic. Oh, I loved how you left me without giving me a kiss good-bye," he says trying to pull a guilt trip on me.

You looked so peaceful, I didn't want to wake you. It was already hard trying to get dressed and talk to Trey without waking you."

"It's all good. I'll remember that," he says turning his back towards me.

"Good! Take a picture," I say jokingly.

He looks back at me with a smile on his face and grabs my hand and says, "Come here." He leads me to the overlook of Kentucky with my hand in his.

"Demonte, after everything we've been through together, I think it's safe to say that we really do love each other, right?"

"Yeah, why? What's up?" I ask in agony.

"Baby, I really, REALLY do love you with all of my heart but there's one thing I must ask you," he says looking me dead in my eyes.

"Carlos, what is it? You're scaring me."

"Just do me a favor and turn around."

As I turn around, I see my mother and brother with Carlos mother with poster boards and as they turn them around it reads out, "Will You Marry…" But marry who though?

But strangely as I turn around to ask Carlos what was going on, he's shorter then he was 20 seconds ago. As I look at him, he has "Me?" written on his forehead.

"Baby, what's going on?" I ask as I feel tears taking over my eyes.

My adrenaline is pumping so much that I begin to shake and I see that Carlos can see and feel it. Am I really being asked to be his husband?

"Demonte, I'm asking you to be my partner, my ace. I can't see my life without you being in it forever," he says reaching into his pocket, "Demonte Durrell Bryant, will you marry me?"

"Carlos, yes, YES, I WILL MARRY YOU!"

Chapter Nineteen

A Night To Remember

Did that really happen yesterday? Did Carlos really to me? TO ME? While replaying the events in my mind, all I can do is smile. He really knows and makes me happy. While pulling into Julia's driveway, I just stare at my ring in amazement because I'm officially engaged to the man of my dreams. After 10 minutes of staring at my finger, my phone knocks me out of my daydream.

"Hello?" I say answering my phone.

"Bra, where are you? We legit got two hours until the party," Julia says sounding angry.

"Girl, I just pulled into your driveway. What's wrong with you?" I ask her concerned.

"My hair ain't coming out right and neither one of you here to help me," she says starting to cry.

"Girl, where you at?" I call out as I let myself in.

"My room," Julia says.

I make a mad dash upstairs to rescue her poor scalp.

"What's the problem?" I ask walking in her room.

"I can't get this part to act right," she says holding the section of hair by her left temple.

"Ok, I'll fix it. That way I can catch you up on me and Carlos," I say holding up my left hand.

"OMG! Demonte, NO!" she screams.

"Demonte, no what?" Brianna asks walking in on the tail end on the conversation.

I show her the ring and they both grab me shouting for joy. I try to act excited but not heard from since last night is bothering me. All of a sudden, the celebration stops.

"What's wrong? Spill the tea, shame the devil," Julia says sitting down passing me a pair of hot flat irons.

"Well, I'm kinda worried about Carlos because I haven't heard from him since last night. I mean he could be busy getting ready for tonight but it just feels funny," I say trying to fix her hair.

"Well look, go try and call him again and I'll take care of this situation," Brianna says taking the flat irons from me.

I give them both a hug, grab my call and go into the hallway.

"Hey, it's Carlos. Sorry, I couldn't make it to the phone but leave a detailed message and I'll return your call as soon as possible. Peace," his voicemail says for the third time in a row.

I try shrugging it off and start getting ready for the party. After three hours of prep and 12 missed calls to Carlos' phone, my nerves are shot through the roof. The party is starting, people are starting to show and I still haven't heard from him.

"This not like him. He would've called, texted, hell even sent an email., but nothing," I say to Julia and Brianna over the loud music.

"He's gonna show. Right, Brianna?" Julia asks as she looks at her for backing.

"Yeah, of course. You guys relationship is starting to go up. Trust me, he'll show. Now stop worrying and enjoy yourself until he does show," she says dancing to 'Work' by Kelly Rowland.

As I look into the crowd, I get this strong vibe, the same strange vibe from the mall, all over again. I call again but this time his voicemail is full.

"Ok, it's official because his voicemail is full," I say as I scan the room.

"You sure it ain't just his phone bugging?" Julia asks while taking a sip of her pop.

"Yeah, I'm sure," I say as I make eye contact with what is making me feel funny.

The last thing that I need to happen right now is officially happening right now. Ryan, of all people, is making his way towards me with a smile.

"Which one of you heffa's invited him?" I ask pointing directly at Ryan.

"Wh-," Brianna starts but stops when she sees him, "what is he doing here?"

"Who?" Julia asks clueless to who we're talking about.

"Ryan!" I shout as he gets closer.

"Ryan from Birmingham Ryan?" she asks putting two and two together.

"Yes, that Ryan."

"Demonte, long time," he says as he approaches us with an evil smirk on his face.

"Ryan, what the hell are you doing here?" Brianna asks as she and Julia stand firmly behind me.

"Question is, who the hell invited you?" Julia asks with every bit of anger.

"I'm Sidney's plus one. But to answer your question Brianna, I'm just here to see if Mr. Bryant knows who Carlos has been with when he's not around?"

"If you're referring to Carlos infidelities, we've both moved on since then," I say, showing him my left hand.

"Aww, that's cute, really cute," Ryan says getting ready to walk away.

"Don't let him get to you," Julia says grabbing my arm.

"Ryan might not get to you, but Carlos will," Brianna says pulling me towards her.

As the force from her grasp my attention towards her direction, I see Carlos staggering in yelling my name.

"Carlos!" I yell running towards him. Carlos, baby, what happened?"

As I grab him, he pulls away from me until he sees that it's me.

"Demonte, I'm so sorry," he cries out faintly.

"Carlos, baby, just tell me what happened."

"Somebody call 911!" I hear somebody scream as the music stops.

As I look at him, I see that his clothes are ripped and bloody while his jean button is broken but is still managing to hold them together.

"HE DID IT!" he says looking up towards Ryan.

When I look up at Ryan, I see a strong presence of evil surround him. With my anger and adrenalin pumping, I charge towards him screaming, "WHAT DID YOU DO TO HIM?! WHAT DID YOU DO TO HIM, YOU BASTARD?!"

But as I make it close to him, everybody tries to hold me back. The pain, the anger, the frustration. All the emotions that he brings feels as they are all multiplied times 10. He is actually getting to me when it was one point and time where he couldn't get under my skin but he is actually succeeding.

"What's wrong, Demonte? Looks as if yo li'l fiancé got jumped," Ryan says sarcastically.

"Demonte, baby, let's just go, please," Carlos faintly says.

I look back at him, "Naw baby, I gotta score to settle for the last time."

Before I know it, I feel a blow from Ryan as I fall to the ground. I feel my face to make sure I'm not bleeding, get up and reach into my back pocket.

"DEMONTE, NO!" I hear Julia scream as I hear gun shots ring out.

Chapter Twenty

Final Destination

Why me? Why did this happen to me? Why did it have to happen at the peak of my life and career? Sitting here in this courtroom is making my blood boil and my heart at the same. Thank God for the support system that I have because having my mother and brother behind me every step of the way and my aunt as my counsel, is making this a whole lot more manageable.

"So, Demonte, I'm trying my hardest to as little to no time here as possible. You just trust me, okay?" my aunt says squeezing my hand.

"Aunt Terry, 15 to life though? At this point, I'm scared, especially considering my life falls into the hands of 12 people," I whisper to her.

As the courtroom grows quiet, I hear the door open behind me. I look back and to my surprise, it's Carlos being escorted in by Julia and Brianna. Brianna and Julia speak while Carlos sends me a kiss. This gives me a sign of relief because through it all, it feels good knowing that the love of my life is here having my back.

But as I think back upon the chain of events, it kills me on the inside knowing that Ryan had him jumped and raped by someone, but by somebody that is HIV/Aids positive. The last time we had a conversation when I was first locked up three months ago, he is terrified that there's a chance that he may have it but won't know until another six months pass to know for sure.

"Ma," I call out silently facing Aunt Terry.

"Yes baby," she says holding back tears.

"Do you have my ring?"

"Yeah, it's right here. Why?" she asks looking in her purse.

"Just give it to Aunt Terry," I say looking all the way back at Carlos.

Like clockwork, she gives it to Trey, he slides it to her. Seeing the ring on my finger, I cannot but only feel the love from my family, my girls and most of all, Carlos.

"Look, whatever happens in this courtroom, I want all y'all to know that I love you guys with all my heart and nothing can change that. I know we've had our differences but the love between us is stronger than ever. I just need to know one thing," I say gently squeezing Aunt Terry's hand.

"What is it?" Aunt Terry asks softly.

Do y'all forgive me for everything? For all the pain and sadness that I've taking y'all through?" I ask as I feel the tears coming. Without an answer, my mother is trying to hold back the tears.

"Bra, no doubt," Trey says holding my mother.

"I wouldn't be here if I didn't. Especially representing you on the house," my aunt says with a smile.

As we pull ourselves together, the door on the front right side opens up with the jury and bailiff walking through.

"Will the defendant, please rise," the judge orders, "Have the jury found a verdict?"

"Yes, we have, your honor," the black juror responds.

"On the count of attempted murder, how do you find the defendant?"

"We, the jury, find Demonte Durrell Bryant...," the juror says drawing a huge silence in the courtroom.

I squeeze my aunts hand so hard that I think that I'm cutting off her circulation and holding my breath at the same time. Will I get 15 years? Or will I have to spend the rest of my life in jail? I still can't understand fully how all of this jumped off and ruin me in every way possible while jeopardizing me in this humiliating and hurtful way. What does God have planned for me at this point in life?

A story as old as times, The Perfect Love Strangers is everything but that, with the perfect twist. Demonte Bryant, the hopless romantic, moves back to his hometown of CIncinnati, with his family (his mother Joy and brother Trey). He starts his new journey optimistic of starting a new life without any trouble from his past life coming back with a vengeance while also hiding a major part of his life from his loved ones. Along the way of rebuilding his new life, his finds new love, friends and starting as a freshman in college, but his old life is up to new tricks to destroy him.

About The Wrighter
Benji The Wrighter originally started out as just a blogger, but expanded into short stories, novels and poetry. With the love and passion for writing and holds a great deal of publishing great bodies of work.

Made in the USA
Columbia, SC
21 June 2024

37082982R00117